THE ZYNE PROJECT

SARA BROOKE

For Shy Gluzman; May the light of your memory remind me of that which I cannot recall

PROLOGUE

The piano music mixed with the air. It sifted through the silence and danced amongst the invisible gentle winds that swept through the palatial mansion. Crystal glasses clinked in the distance, followed by laughter augmented by the blushing freeness of intoxication, while outside, a warm breeze flowed freely through the palm trees and exited out toward the southern skies.

She walked quickly through the halls, her high heels clicking as they swept across marble floors. Gentle lights glittered from the chandeliers hanging overhead. As the door to her bedroom approached, she increased her pace, quickly reaching out to grasp the bronze door handle and escape inside.

Once in her room, she removed the now-quite-uncomfortable shoes and dress, choosing to sit in front of the vanity mirror wearing only lace thong underwear and a matching strapless bra. The vision that stared back was most impressive to many and certainly to the majority who were attending the dinner party.

But it didn't look the same way to its owner.

Slowly, the woman began running her fingers through her hair, looking almost distracted as her vision seemed to glaze over. Sinking deeper into her thoughts, she furrowed her brow and began to push elegant fingertips through ebony hair.

As time quickly ticked by, she pushed her fingers harder and harder against her scalp until each motion was more of a scratch...

She began to pull her hair out. Piece by piece she continued yanking out strands, while scratching her scalp, causing it to bleed. Crimson stained skin lodged itself under her fingernails as the act continued, again and again. She tugged and mutilated herself for twenty minutes until she realized that her ten-year-old son was standing in the doorway, watching.

"Mom, what are you doing? What are you doing?"

CHAPTER 1

D r. Dan Johns was exhausted. He'd been standing over a microscope for hours and alternately punching formulas into a PC that seemed to be working more slowly by the minute. Testing had taken him nearly nineteen hours straight, but after many months—he had finally figured it out.

The directive given to him by the Zyne Corporation was top-secret and anything that confidential usually meant he wouldn't have many people to rely on and every move he made would have to be documented. Despite his reputation as an astute medical doctor and esteemed scientist, Dan felt like he had to continuously prove himself to the major manufacturers that courted and eventually retained him for assistance. That had been the protocol pretty much ever since he decided to allow himself to solicit for outside work, while still treating patients part-time at the University of Southeast Florida.

When Zyne came his way, the proposal was one of the most exciting he'd ever heard. They wanted him to conduct research using a new concoction they'd created in theory—and needed him to help make the formula a reality.

Zyne specialized in hair products. Gels, hairsprays, shampoos, and conditioners—they were involved in all of it. But their president and CEO had greater aspirations. It was his dream…his desire…to fundamentally *change* the choices people had when it came to hair. He wanted to give people the choice to pick the type of hair color they wanted and not be shackled by what they were born with. By changing hair color, the hope was that the formula, once created, would also be able to change the consistency of the hair. So, in essence, a person could choose to have thick black hair or fine blonde hair.

It was a concept that had long been discussed by genetic engineering experts globally, but never fully realized.

Not until now.

Dan took the information derived by Zyne researchers and reviewed what he knew about hair pigment types: Eumelanin, which causes black or brown hair, Pheomelanin that creates red hair color, and the loss of these melanocytes, which causes gray hair. He studied the pigments and the variations of hair color created through different levels of each. But then, he dug further into the genetics of hair color and the alleles involved and discovered that by isolating those genes within a special mixture, he could deliver a genetic cocktail through an infusion. This infusion contained a weakened virus that carried the hair genes to the cells of the recipient.

Tests took months. But finally—on a rainy dark Friday evening, Dan saw what his eyes could not quite comprehend at first. The infusion had worked on a small laboratory mouse that was greedily eating a morsel of cheese. Only, the mouse was no longer white.

It was auburn.

CHAPTER 2

Traffic was awful, but Rosa Rodriguez managed to find her way to the Illusions building, despite the hidden sign and remote location. Directions had been emailed to her by the Zyne Public Relations Director, but she was unfamiliar with the area and hence, found them difficult to follow. The roads this far west were much different than the heavily traveled routes in downtown Miami. There, Rosa felt much more at ease. But here, passing through heavily wooded roads, she worried about hitting some strange, wild animal making the unfortunate decision to cross the street.

Zyne chose to conduct its human clinical trials at the Illusions building for many reasons. The primary one being that it belonged to the company, and had been used before due to its secluded nature, and the ability for test subjects to basically live at the facility during the duration of the trial, enjoying the amenities provided while essentially standing in as human guinea pigs. Granted, that wasn't how the Zyne people positioned it, but Rosa wasn't dumb. She knew that you could dress it up all you wanted, but in the end, you were still getting stuck, prodded, and tested for *their* benefit...not yours.

She needed to be here. There were rumblings throughout the higher ranks at the CDC that this trial was not entirely safe and had been allowed due to the influence and powerful financiers of the company. It was no secret that Zyne contributed heavily to politicians who were very influential in the decision making that affected the FDA and associated agencies.

After reading the reams of paperwork available through the CDC about gene therapy, Rosa agreed to become a part of the month-long experiment and keep an eye on progress. It wasn't a commonly publicized assignment, but whenever experimental therapies were tested on humans, the government managed to get involved.

And this truly was experimental. The test subjects weren't common laboratory rats. Chuckling to herself, Rosa thought about the group she was about to join. Far from small, helpless animals, this group represented some of the most wealthy, popular people in the country.

Upon discovering that the formula, called "Z", was actually working, a very strategic recruitment process had begun. Invitations to participate were given to an exclusive group of people who wanted to change the color of their hair and were prominent enough to be considered for the trial. These weren't common men and women—but rather, the elite—given the opportunity to participate in a life-changing event—the ability to change their hair color...permanently.

Pulling around the long circular driveway that led to the Illusions building, Rosa mentally recited the names of the other subjects in her head. The first was Tim Drake, one of the world's most accomplished surfers who would be joined by Bryan Jackson, an NBA all-star and Rick Danzer, a billionaire hair products tycoon. The women included Jennifer Blazer, a socialite extraordinaire with long blonde hair and legs to match and Teresa Lee, the multi-millionaire owner of a travel website.

And then, there was Rosa.

Zyne executives had reluctantly allowed Rosa to join the group because of her government status, but she was given specific instructions before arriving to keep her identity private. She should masquerade as a famous surgeon who was lucky enough to have been chosen given her ability to utilize the "Z" technology on recovering cancer patients who had completed chemotherapy and were able to grow their hair back. With this new treatment, she could offer them the chance to grow their hair in any color they wanted.

The story seemed a little far-fetched to her, because what recovering cancer patient who had just been through numerous infusions would want another one? But she didn't have time to argue because she wanted this assignment and would do what was needed to make it work. The only way for a woman to rise through the ranks was to take chances. Rosa, a self-proclaimed workaholic, wasn't going to pass up the opportunity to make her mark.

She parked her car and looked around. The Illusions building was comprised of three different shaped structures connected together in a long snake-like fashion. The main central building was two stories with the other two at ground level. All participants had been warned that to ensure privacy and security from the media, extreme measures had been taken to keep things private. Those measures hadn't been detailed in the contract, but she knew that could mean outside security, immediate lock-down, and swift legal action to anyone who tried to breach the perimeter.

Stepping out of the car, she looked at what would be her home for the next few weeks. On the outside, the compound was painted a stark white, but once inside, was extremely well furnished and had the look and feel of a luxury resort.

Rosa knew that was part of the plan. In order to keep the high-maintenance guests comfortable, they would enjoy spa-like amenities during the day. The trial would require all subjects to shave their heads so that the newer hair could grow in as desired. And while they waited for their hair to grow back, massages, facials, and other spa treatments would commence.

"Hello," a manicured blonde said, greeting Rosa as she approached what appeared to be a reception desk. "I hope you found the building ok. It really is in the middle of nowhere." The blonde chuckled to herself and proceeded to gather all of Rosa's information, while motioning for a uniformed man nearby to take the bags. She stopped smiling and stared at Rosa with stony blue eyes, "Please understand, we will need to take your cell phone and all personal belongings. This study is extremely confidential and we need to ensure that all of our guests are in controlled surroundings. Are you ok with these terms?"

Rosa wasn't sure she felt good about giving up all of her communication to the outside world, but figured if she said no, she might be on her way out. So she agreed and handed over her cell phone and keys.

"Thanks! Ok, now please sign this paperwork. This just covers what you already know...that your head is going to be shaved in preparation... that you will be infused twice a day with a gene-therapy solution... that you may feel a bit sick or have a reaction..."

The woman went on and on and Rosa felt her stomach turn as she reviewed the lengthy paperwork that basically allowed Zyne to shoot her up with whatever solution the scientists had created, whether or not it made her sick. With shaking hands she signed the document and was escorted to her second floor room by the uniformed bellman. Before he departed, he mentioned that dinner would be at six o'clock, and she would have a chance to meet everyone else at that time.

Sitting on the bed, Rosa looked around and barely saw the elegance of her posh new home. Instead, her stomach hurt and she wondered if perhaps she had made the wrong decision.

Why had he decided to do this?

That was the question Bryan asked himself while filling out reams of paperwork at the front desk while a hot-yet-idiotic blonde smiled at him with the whitest teeth he'd ever seen. But he knew the answer to his own frustrated question.

It was the gray.

He *hated* his gray hair. Absolutely, positively hated it. And it didn't make him feel any better that all the men in his family had prematurely grayed as well. Bottom line was he still had a nice head of hair, but the damn thing was so full of gray that he chose to shave his head rather than color it regularly. It was just a frustrating, aggravating mess. So when his agent called and told him that there was the possibility of fixing his hair problem with some new type of gene therapy, and he was eligible to participate since it was during his off-season, Bryan jumped at the opportunity. It was the chance of a lifetime and if there was anyone who was going to benefit from this stuff, it was him.

Finalizing his registration, he noticed a familiar face approaching the desk. He recognized Jennifer from the trash tabloid magazines his girlfriends were always bringing over. From the stuff he'd read, Jennifer Blazer was one of the richest women in Los Angeles—an heiress of some sort. But he also knew she was bad news and always getting into trouble. So he smiled when she approached but quickly turned and headed toward his room.

He could feel her watching him as he strode out of the lobby, and quickened his pace as he headed for the upstairs sleeping quarters.

Jennifer was annoyed. Why did it always seem like people disrespected her? She recognized Bryan right away. Hell, anyone would. He was all over Sports Illustrated and was one of the most talented basketball players in the NBA. Sighing, she dropped her purse on the counter and started the lengthy registration process. When the smiling blonde behind the counter mentioned that she would have to give up her cell phone, she seriously re-considered.

Do I really want to do this? She thought. *What if something happens? How am I supposed to handle the next month without my phone?*

The woman rambled on about how there would be breaks within the next five weeks when guests could use their phones, but for now, all communication would have to be terminated given the sensitive nature of the trial. It hurt, but Jennifer did turn over her phone. Feeling like a desolate child and a bit helpless, she allowed herself to be escorted to her room.

Once inside and alone, she looked out the window. The location was remote, surrounded by large trees and a forest that seemed to stretch for miles. All the excitement about becoming a redhead and making a huge publicity splash disappeared and was replaced by anxiety. Still, Jennifer knew that this stunt would help her recover what had become a tarnished image over the years.

She was only twenty-two, but had slept with many famous and infamous men. Somehow, the paparazzi always managed to find out who she was fucking and proceeded to hound her and the unlucky bastard nonstop, taking a million photographs and painting her face across the cover of trash tabloid magazines.

Her break-ups were the worst. Unable to control a somewhat short temper, Jennifer was often photographed screaming at a new ex, her face contorted in senseless rage.

This trial was a chance to be a part of something different. She would be taking steps in an unknown direction…changing the face of science…

But something didn't feel right. She couldn't put her finger on it, but somehow she didn't trust these people. Everyone she'd met smiled and said the right things, but she was uneasy about shaving her head and putting her life in the hands of the nurses and staff who got their paychecks from Zyne.

It all seemed too good to be true. The ability to change her hair color to something she'd always wanted. The ability to start over. It sounded so enticing…

So why was she so nervous?

CHAPTER 3

D an paced up and down the floor. His "guests" were sitting in chairs, their arms resting comfortably while the liquid from their infusions crept through tubes and into their arms.

Dinner had been good. The subjects had gotten to know each other and seemed to get along. Upon closer assessment, he was pleased with the decision they'd made to bring these six people together for what would be one of the most groundbreaking studies ever.

If…things went well.

There had been a few glitches since the successful mice infusions. For one, the mice seemed *different* after the infusions. They were not as frightened of people and were more confident when handled and studied. But some of the mice had become more aggressive, and one had even bit one of the researchers before it was euthanized. Dan wasn't too concerned because the majority of the test mice seemed fine, but the fact remained that they weren't allowed to live long enough for him to do lengthy research. Once their fur grew in, he'd been instructed to kill them in order to study their blood and organs to ensure that nothing had been damaged in the process.

The good news was that their organs appeared fine, but he'd fought with Zyne to give him more time to observe the mice before testing on humans.

Despite his arguments, he'd been overruled by other scientists who felt that studies on humans would be fine. After all, gene therapy was different than other types of pills or solutions given orally or intravenously. There were few deaths or complications for most similar-type studies and given that the gene was "hair" related and not tied to tumors or other more dangerous conditions, there was an assumption that it would either work or not work—and at very little risk to the participants.

But now, a pang of fear shot through his skull. *What if the infusion doesn't work?* he thought. *What if nothing happens?*

"Dr. Johns, how are you?" chirped one of the patients, interrupting his thoughts. He walked over to Jennifer and watched as the infusion dripped down the clear tubing into her arm.

"I'm doing fine. Hi, Jennifer. How are you feeling?"

He watched as she managed a small smile. The overhead lights glinted off her bald head. She'd cried when medical personnel had shaved her scalp, but now seemed a bit better.

"I'm ok. It just feels weird to be bald and my arm stings a bit."

He reached down and gently touched her shoulder. "Don't worry, this infusion causes hair to grow back more quickly. From what I understand, you're getting the redhead formula and that one does seem to encourage hair growth."

She nodded.

"Yeah, don't worry. In a few days, you'll start to see those red sprouts come in and you'll be very happy…trust me."

Jennifer smiled at him and seemed to relax.

Walking over to some of the other subjects, he was relieved to see that they all appeared calm and content. Rosa and Teresa were discussing the latest national politics while they both received their therapy. From what he understood, both brunettes were receiving blonde infusions. He smiled at them and walked over to check on the men.

The male subjects all seemed relaxed with the exception of the hair products tycoon, Rick, who fidgeted anxiously and took annoyed deep breaths every once in a while. Thinking back, Dan remembered that Rick had been invited to join the study because he was one of the largest distributors of off-label Zyne products. He'd created some of his own brands over the years, but was a close "friend" of Zyne's CEO and continued to provide global outlets for cheaper brands—some literally made out of perfumed soap and water.

"Hey, doctor..." Rick said in a thick New York accent, "When's this gonna start working? I mean, how long does it take for the genes to kick in?"

Smiling politely, Dan attempted to explain that once his hair grew back, it would grow in with the color and consistency of the formula being infused. Rick, who was balding, could expect to see dark brown hair emerge within a week or so and would hopefully see a fuller head of hair as well.

Rick nodded in appreciation and leaned back in his chair. He turned away from the doctor and concentrated on the sports event unfolding on one of the TVs that hung overhead.

Satisfied that Rick was more comfortable, Dan looked around and saw that his two athletes, Tim and Bryan were talking about sports, while the gene therapy dripped into their arms.

Confident that everyone was stable, Dan headed for his makeshift office when his cell phone rang.

"Hello?"

"Hi, Dan." The voice on the phone sounded concerned. It was his assistant, April.

"Hey what's up, April? How are our smaller subjects doing?" he asked jokingly. April was aware of the type of clientele Zyne had recruited and often commented that she was happy *he* was the one handling the trial.

But now, she sounded concerned. "Dan, there's something wrong with the twins."

The "twins" were two mice that spent an inordinate amount of time together. Despite being in a testing environment with a number of other creatures, the furry companions were constantly together. The scientists at the laboratory had affectionately named them "the twins", despite one now being a brunette and the other a blonde. The mice had been infused several weeks back and now proudly displayed their new fur colors. Unfortunately, they would be destroyed in a few weeks, but some of the technicians had discussed possibly taking them home as pets.

"What's wrong?"

"Well, they seem to be changing..." April hesitated, "For starters, they're losing their fur. We're not sure why that's happening. It could just be that they're nervous or have an infection. There's something else—their faces are contorting. It seems as if their muscular structure is altered somehow."

Dan's heart was beating fast. "How are the other mice?"

"The other mice are fine," she answered, "No problems other than the fact that some of them have been displaying aggression, but nothing vastly different than before. Dan, do you think maybe we should stop the trial? These recent changes are worrisome. At least to me. What do you think?"

Dan turned and looked back at the subjects who were already receiving their first infusions.

"Not sure we can stop now. Let me see what the people at Zyne say."

Dan's discussion with Zyne representatives did not go well. They demanded to know how many animals had been affected, and when Dan reported that only two mice out of several hundred were experiencing hair loss and personality changes, their reaction wasn't what he'd hoped for.

"Let's see how our folks do," he was told. "It's a trial after all. They know the risks. If things start getting out of hand, we'll shut it down. But for now, let's stay the course. We've just started and need to see how things go."

When the phone call ended, Dan felt uneasy and he wondered about how much of a risk the Zyne Corporation was willing to take.

The massage was invigorating. Teresa couldn't remember the last time she had been so relaxed. The masseuse manipulated her muscles and expertly worked out the tension. Warm oils were lathered all over her body and as the world continued to melt away, she thought about her life.

Things had been rough lately. The breakup with Jean-Paul had been difficult enough, but to top it off, her business was struggling due to issues with the airlines and inconsistencies with listed rates. The past few quarters the site had posted large losses and her accountants were starting to get nervous.

Doctors said her alopecia was a result of stress and lack of sleep.

But Teresa knew better. She simply had to stop pulling her hair out during times of stress.

Sometimes she forgot about it. She'd be sitting at her desk at work, and while thinking about how much there was to do, start gently yanking on strands of her long black hair. If no one noticed, she might be pulling on it for hours. Over time however, the constant yanking and tugging created bald spots that she could not hide. So, when her business partner mentioned a study that could change the consistency and color of her hair, Teresa thought it would be a great idea. What better way to end her nervous habit than to first shave her head and then allow new, more beautiful hair to grow in.

Since her head had been shaved that morning, she'd felt the addictive impulse to once again pull on her hair. But without any tufts protruding from her scalp, it was just an unsatisfied burning urge—an invisible itch that she could not scratch. So, instead of thinking about it, she succumbed to the massage and tried to focus on thoughts that were pleasant.

Teresa was just starting to relax, when a sharp pang of pain suddenly hit her, like a spike being shoved directly through her skull.

Sitting up quickly, she sent the masseuse spiraling backwards. "Oh!" she apologized, "I'm so sorry. My head just started hurting all of a sudden."

The masseuse asked if she wanted to call for medical assistance, but Teresa declined. "No, that's ok. Let's just finish the massage. It feels so good, I would hate for you to have to stop."

Lying back down on the table, Teresa took a few ·deep breaths but the pain lingered. She closed her eyes and tried not to think about it.

At the same time, the others in the group decided to take a swim in the outdoor heated pool. Sporting bald heads and towels, Tim joked that they looked like a bunch of "cone heads" from another planet. The group chuckled, but everyone was secretly relieved to be done with the first infusion.

The pool, located on the east wing of the building was kidney shaped and surrounded by tables and chairs. Colorful foliage encapsulated the entire area, giving visitors the impression of being transported to a tropical paradise. Bright blue water reflected the glowing orb of the sun and gently rippled from the jets of water shooting out underneath the surface.

Tim and Bryan immediately jumped into the pool, while Rosa and Jennifer sprawled out on the lounge chairs. Rick was pacing the deck, looking irritated.

Tim tossed his head back and basked in the warmth of the sun. He didn't mind being bald. It felt kind of cool and he was looking forward to having sun-kissed blonde hair that didn't have to come from a bottle. Tim had been secretly bleaching his hair for years, but the media and his fans always talked about his golden locks as a birthright. His hair was actually a mousey brown and despite the sun's bleaching effects, it took many regular visits to the salon to keep the public's distorted perception alive. In addition, he was approaching thirty-five and knew that his years in the spotlight were finite. This was his one chance to look good again and change history—at least for a little while.

He was also thinking about his financial situation. A hidden, but growing gambling problem had drained his bank accounts. Too many underground poker games were taking their toll on his nest egg and most of the money he'd made from sponsors as he tackled the waves was slowly draining out of a sieve held in a viselike grip by people who were rumored to be connected to the mafia. The problem was they made it very easy for him to drop-in on a running poker or blackjack game that never ended. It was easy access to an addiction that held him firmly by the balls.

And they know it too, he thought grimly.

After months and months of losses, Tim owed quite a bit of money. And he knew that time was running out. If he could emerge from all of this as a bigger star than before, it might lead to some extra cash.

Maybe even a movie deal…

It might save my life…

Tim shook off his fears and plunged his head into the water again. When he emerged, he shook his skull back and forth to shake off the droplets of water and howled like a deranged wolf.

Several members of the group laughed, but Rick glared at the surfer from the other end of the pool deck and closed his eyes in annoyance.

Rick had barely ever heard of Tim before this ordeal and was an elitist who didn't mind being a snob. He felt like he was classier than his fellow subjects and the idea that he couldn't communicate via a cell phone was driving him nuts.

"Yo, Rick. What's wrong dude?" Tim asked.

As patiently as he could, Rick took a deep breath and answered, "I'm fine. Just have a lot going on with the business, so kind of irritated that we can't use our phones. Don't see what the big deal is."

Tim laughed, "Man, you just need to chill. Why don't you grab a chair and some drinks and we'll all wait for our crazy hair to grow in."

Rick huffed in irritation and strode back inside, leaving the group laughing at his departure.

Needing a break from the hot sun, Rosa stood up from the lounge chair and walked over to the deep end of the pool, diving straight in. When her body hit the water, she felt a sharp pain in her head and for a split second thought she saw something strange. It looked like a dark mass by the shallow end. She immediately backed up and lifted her head quickly out of the water. From the surface everything looked fine, so she ducked her head under again and squinted to see.

There was nothing there.

As she lifted her head above water, she tried to re-engage in the discussion, but was frightened by her hallucination. Her headache wasn't powerful, but it was definitely lingering. Dan and the others in charge of the trial mentioned that there would be some side effects from the mild virus used in the infusion such as headache, dizziness, and nausea. But he hadn't said anything about hallucinations. Stepping out of the pool and grabbing a towel, she looked over at the shallow end one final time, gazing at the glittering rays of sunlight glinting off the water.

The group met up for dinner that evening, a few hours after their second infusion. Everyone was now feeling fatigued and a little sick, which had been expected. The meal was intentionally light; consisting of vegan pasta, thinly sliced deli meat, and salads. Plates were filled halfway and most of the discussions centered on fatigue and the continual, though somewhat muted excitement over how their hair would grow in.

Jennifer pushed her pasta around the plate and yawned without covering her mouth. She was bored and wanted to be out with her friends. Not having her cell phone was irritating and her body felt weird. She wasn't sure she could stand weeks and weeks of this torture and for the first time since she'd arrived, thought about leaving.

But that wasn't an option. The group had been surprised and slightly frightened to discover that the Illusions building was locked up each night—from the outside. There was no way out as the doors locked automatically at ten o'clock, and the entire perimeter was now filled with guards on patrol to ensure that the media could not get in. Word had already leaked that the high profile group was involved in something ground breaking and media was camped by the entrance of the compound doing live shots and waiting for some word about what was happening.

Where else could you find such power players all together and kept hidden for so long?

––––––––––

Rosa knew that the formula was working its way through their bodies and wondered what the side effects would be. She'd caught the scientist, Dan, staring at all of them carefully throughout the day as if to see if anything was awry. Clearly that was part of the observation, but he seemed a bit high strung. She tried to engage him in conversation.

"So, Dr. Johns, how do you think we're doing so far?" she asked casually, spooning a ream of spaghetti into her mouth. He seemed pensive but smiled back at her.

"Rosa, I think you guys are doing great. I know you must be missing your family..." he hesitated, realizing his mistake. All subjects had been chosen because of their single or divorced status and none of them had children. This was done on purpose to reduce possible security breaches. He also knew that Rosa was divorced, lived alone, and worked for the CDC, so he would need to be careful when dealing with her.

She didn't seem to care that he'd made the inadvertent insensitive comment and smiled back, "Not really. My parents don't live nearby, and I work so much that relationships have to take a back seat. But, you know that already Dr. Johns, don't you?" she winked.

Dan was trying to return with a clever rebuttal, but their conversation was cut short because Rick was now standing up and swaying back and forth. He looked positively green.

"Uhhh...I don't feel so good..." he muttered and lurched forward, vomiting his salad all over the table. The green liquid shot out in all directions, drenching the table in a smelly, oily mess. The others gagged and pushed their chairs back to avoid suffering the same fate.

Teresa failed and ended up vomiting up her dinner as well.

Dan jumped up and quickly motioned for the nurses to help Rick and Teresa back to their rooms. Ushering the others into a common area that contained sofas and a large screen TV, he paused for a moment—contemplating how to address the group. Meanwhile, the remaining patients chattered amongst themselves, disgusted by what they'd just seen.

"Dude, that was nasty!" Tim was saying, "I mean, I don't feel all that great either, but you don't see me barfing all over everything. It's like, find a bathroom or something man...don't make the rest of us sick."

Jennifer agreed. "Yeah, it's bad enough they have us locked up in here, but to have to smell and see that? Totally gross."

Dan sighed and addressed the group once they'd all quieted down. "Look," he started, "I know you're all feeling pretty rough right now. It's a side effect of the infusion and the viruses we've had to inject you with to carry the hair genes to your cells. You will start to feel better in a few days. I think it might be best if you all go to bed early tonight and get some rest. It's been a long first day."

Everyone agreed and the bald subjects dispersed, each heading to their own room. Once inside his room, Tim ran to the bathroom and vomited up his dinner into the toilet. He'd hidden it from the others, but felt really bad. Almost as if someone was pulling his skull apart in two different directions.

Lying down on his bed, he closed his eyes and fell asleep. While he slept, a small bulge formed on his neck and a trickle of blood seeped out of his right ear.

———————————

Back in her room, Rosa sat on a chair near the window and stared out at the darkening sky. She listened to the wind whistle through the branches as the trees surrounding the compound swayed back and forth in a hypnotic fashion. Putting her head to the cool glass, she thought about what Dan had said to her earlier in the evening.

Rosa's immediate family lived in San Antonio, Texas. Her father had died when she was very young, leaving her mother to fend for three children. Rosa's childhood had been a mixture of constant hunger, embarrassment, and poverty. When opportunities in life came calling, she couldn't wait to leave it all behind.

She'd stood fully packed at the front door, waiting to step out into a new future. Her mother had given her a strong hug and wept silently. It had been painful and once Rosa left—she never looked back.

Now, sitting alone, she reflected on the price she was paying for her solid, unwavering desire to succeed. She'd only had two serious relationships in the past, and both lasted only one year before her relentless drive and career determination destroyed the path to love.

She knew what it was like to be alone. And normally it didn't bother her.

Sighing, she stood up and wiped the tears that had stealthily emerged from the corners of her eyes and were now dripping down her cheeks.

Pull it together, Rosa, she thought.

CHAPTER 4

The next few days were similar and unexpectedly difficult on the group. Each person gave blood in the morning for testing and then sat through the first infusion of the day. Then, it was free time to enjoy the pool, a massage, a facial, or a book in the shade. In the afternoon, the second infusion was given and then it was time for dinner, some TV, and bed. Everyone was tired by nine o'clock and despite some of them being night owls under normal circumstances, there wasn't a soul awake after midnight.

Things were starting to happen—much to Dan's delight. Jennifer's bald head was now covered with bright orange-red stubble and the rest of the group was exhibiting similar growth.

There were some concerns, however. Tim had developed small cysts under his skin. The lumps first appeared on his neck and were starting to spread down his back. Dan wasn't sure if it was a reaction to the infusion or just a skin condition, so he was keeping a close eye on it. The surfer seemed ok and never complained, but Dan wasn't taking any chances and advised the nursing staff to watch out for any strange behavior.

Teresa was also under observation. Her hair wasn't growing in as fast as the others and upon close examination, one of the nurses noticed that her scalp had scrape marks and red bumps indicating that she had been picking at her stubble. Dan was very aware of this nervous tendency also known as Trichotillomania.

He tried to speak with Teresa about her habit, but she wouldn't listen and just mumbled about the stress of the study. It was important for him to get her to stop yanking her hair out or they wouldn't be able to see if the infusion was working.

As for Bryan and Rick, both seemed stable. Still, it was hard to tell. The men kept to themselves, and Rick had developed a strange cough that he blamed on asthma. Dan assigned a nurse to keep an eye on both of them and report back if anything weird started happening.

When he checked in on Rosa, she appeared to be the only one who was tolerating the infusion, so he left her alone.

Dan was wrong.

Rosa felt awful. Her muscles ached and she'd noticed a strange lump on her back. It hadn't been there the day before, but after a long, dreamless night, she awoke to find a strange, mushy mass on the right side of her upper back. It didn't hurt, but everything else did. Her face, her head, her arms…

Is this normal? she wondered, walking outside to sit by the pool. As she exited out of the cool air-conditioned building, she noticed that Rick was sitting at the far end of the pool on a lounge chair. But he was not relaxing and enjoying the sun. He was fully clothed, holding his head between his hands and rocking back and forth.

Is he moaning?

She got closer and was horrified to see that a river of liquid was seeping through his hands and had created a small pool on the concrete underneath his head.

"Rick?" she asked softly, putting her hand on his shoulder.

He didn't move and just kept rocking back and forth.

"Rick?" she asked again, "Honey, let's get you inside and have one of the nurses take a look at you…"

At the mention of the nurses, Rick dropped his hands and swung his head to look at Rosa.

She backed away when their eyes locked.

Rick's face looked like it was coming unglued. A growing grayish fissure had appeared in the center of his forehead and was separating his face into two distinct pieces. Ooze dripped out and leaked down his nose and lips. His tongue hung from his mouth and his eyes appeared glossed over.

"Helllp mee…" he moaned and reached for Rosa. Horrified, she backed up even though she knew he needed help. She turned and fled out of the pool area, running into the building, desperately searching for a nurse. She finally found one in the dining area.

"We need help. Rick's outside and he's doing really bad. He's really sick. Something's wrong with him…" she babbled hysterically.

The nurse sat her down and asked gently, "Where is he, Rosa?"

"He's outside. I'll show you!" and she leapt up out of the chair, heading for the door. Bryan and Jennifer, overhearing the commotion, joined them.

Rosa threw the doors open, but Rick was gone. The pool area was empty.

"He was here…" she said frustrated, "I saw him. He was sitting right there by the pool. Look, you can still see the puddle he made over there."

The liquid had begun to dry in the overwhelming heat of the afternoon, but it was enough for the nurse to believe what Rosa had witnessed.

"Ok, let's all go inside. I need to find Dr. Johns."

Dan couldn't believe what he was hearing. One of his subjects was having a major reaction and had disappeared somewhere within the building.

And there was no way to find him, other than to search the entire perimeter.

There were many concessions Dan made before beginning the study and one of them was allowing the trial to be conducted without video recording. Due to the nature of the high-profile subjects and the fear that closed-circuit videotaping could potentially be used against them if the tapes were ever stolen, he had agreed to shut down all of the security cameras.

So, there was no recording to help track down Rick. And he could be dying—or worse.

Dan pulled the group together and could see that the trial subjects looked worried. Somehow, he had to try to keep their stress levels manageable given their fragile conditions. But he had some very bad news to share and no matter how he put it, they would not take it well.

"Guys, please try to relax. I've got to talk to you. We've got someone missing…"

The subjects murmured amongst themselves and Dan had to quiet the group down to continue.

"Look, Rick is missing. Rosa saw him by the pool, and he wasn't doing too well. She went to get help, but by the time she got back, he was gone. Has anyone seen him?"

No one had seen Rick since earlier in the day. Taking a deep breath, Dan spoke again, this time very slowly, "Look everyone. I had to report Rick's disappearance and there is a very specific protocol for this kind of situation. We don't know what we're dealing with here and in order to protect all of you and ensure he doesn't harm himself and others, we've locked down the building. That means, we're all stuck here until we can find him."

Jennifer exploded, "What do you mean we're in lockdown? That's bullshit! What if something's wrong with him? And we're all stuck in this building with nowhere to go? You need to let us out, now!"

Dan stared at her with tired eyes, "You want to leave? Don't forget, there's a ton of media outside and you're basically *bald*. Not to mention, you're full of liquid treatment that if we simply stop now, could seriously endanger your health. You sure you want to leave, Jennifer?"

She glared at him and sat down in a huff. Tim, who was sitting quietly, began rubbing his head. "Dude," he said, "I'm not feeling good either. What's wrong with us, doc?"

Dan sat down and leveled with them. "Look, I know you don't feel great, but you're all making medical history and when this study is complete, you're going to walk out of here with your genetics changed forever. Trust me, I want to get you through this trial safely and quickly, but the first thing we need to do is find Rick. Then, we can figure out how to finish your treatments in the safest way possible. Will you help me with this?"

The group looked at each other and reluctantly agreed.

"Ok," said Dan, "Let's break up into groups and search the perimeter. I think groups of three should be fine and then we'll meet back here in the common area in one hour. Sound good?"

Rosa, Bryan, and Jennifer agreed to stay on the first floor and search the rooms including the medical center. Tim, Teresa, and Dan took the elevator up to the second floor to check the rooms upstairs.

"This sucks," Tim moaned as the elevator doors shut and they began to ascend. He leaned up against the wall and grabbed his head with both hands, continuing to moan. Dan moved closer to the surfer.

"What's hurting you Tim?" he asked as the elevator reached the second floor and they all stepped out.

Tim didn't say anything, just shuffled out and suddenly sank to his knees while gripping his head. "It huuurts..." he groaned. Then, he collapsed to the ground in one heavy movement, falling face forward. Dan ran over and tried to touch him, but suddenly, the surfer flung out his arm and knocked him back.

Rising from the ground, the bald man looked crazed. His face was bright red, eyes rolling crazily in their sockets, and a maniacal grin on his face. He stumbled and lurched toward Teresa, who jumped back and ran down the hallway.

Dan regained his balance and chased after them. Tim managed to corner Teresa against a locked door that she was desperately trying to open. He was leaning in and grasping for her repeatedly as she tried to shrink away. Ropes of drool were now hanging out of his mouth and he continued moaning in a nonsensical, psychotic manner.

Dan knew he didn't have much choice, so he reached for the first thing he could find—a ceramic flowerpot. He threw the pot at Tim, who was knocked momentarily off balance. When the madman turned around, he snarled and raced forward.

With his lips peeled back in a bestial grin and eyes glaring, Tim leapt on top of Dan and snapped his teeth together over and over, as if trying to tear skin off the bone. The two men struggled and Dan knew it was key to keep his attacker from biting his face. He managed to flip Tim over on his back and with one hand held him by the throat, while his other hand found a shard of the pot lying nearby. Quickly grasping the sharp weapon, he did the only thing he could think of and stabbed Tim in the throat, tearing it open, revealing arteries and muscle.

Blood shot straight out of the wound and sprayed Dan's face, as if a hose had been turned on at full stream. The struggling weakened and then ceased as the life flowed out of the dying surfer who whimpered, trying to draw in oxygen, but who was now drowning in blood. Finally, Tim gasped and stilled.

Dan fell back and sat on the ground in shock.

What just happened? he thought.

Tim's erratic, maniacal behavior seemed to have come out of nowhere. One moment he was calm and coherent—the next minute—completely crazed.

Teresa was cowering against the door, sobbing as she leaned on the frame. Dan went over and gently pulled her into his arms. Her stubbly head prickled his chin as she leaned against him and shook in terror and despair.

———

Downstairs, the trio assigned to check the common and medical areas were preparing for their search. Bryan was already irritated because Jennifer's babbling was driving him crazy.

"...this is totally ridiculous," she was saying to Rosa, "We shouldn't be stuck here with some sick guy running around. Obviously, there's something wrong. They should just let us out and cancel the study."

31

Bryan whipped his head around and glared at the socialite, "Did you not hear the man? He said that our bodies can't simply stop taking the infusion. We've got to finish what's been started or we could all get really sick. What's wrong with you?"

Jennifer glared and shot back, "There's nothing wrong with me, asshole. I'm just tired and think we deserve answers. This Nancy Drew detective bullshit is ridiculous in my opinion."

Bryan didn't care to argue with her any further, so he tried to be diplomatic. "Look, you don't have to search with us. Why don't you just stay in the lounge, and we'll meet you back here in a little bit?"

Jennifer agreed to stay behind and went in search for something to snack on. When she was out of earshot, Bryan took a deep breath and let it out slowly. "Damn, thought she'd never leave. What a monumental pain in the ass."

Rosa smiled, "Yeah, she's difficult alright, but we have bigger problems right now. Let's go check out the medical center."

The medical center was a large maze of rooms and cubicles where researchers set up their equipment to review test results, met to discuss next steps, and conducted all laboratory work. The duo felt that it was a good place to start their search since it was a relatively large area and contained many corridors where a person could sneak off and hide.

The center was closed off to the rest of the facility by large metal doors marked "Secure Location – Medical Personnel Only."

Bryan reached out to open the doors when suddenly, a plethora of jarring sounds filled the air from beyond the metal barrier.

The sounds of people running, screaming, and bumping into things were crystal clear...even from outside the center.

Bryan and Rosa instinctively backed away from the doors and waited for people to come flying out in a mad rush.

But no one ran out. Instead, the screaming continued, followed by loud thumps and the sound of furniture and glass crashing to the floor.

They both stood motionless and waited. Ten minutes ticked by and the commotion finally stopped, followed by an eerie stillness.

Bryan and Rosa looked at each other and an unspoken agreement passed between them. It was time to go in and face the storm that had just blown through.

They pushed the doors open.

Inside, the lights flickered. It looked like a hurricane had hit. Papers and folders littered the floor in all directions. A strange silence filled the space like a heavy fog, filling them both with an almost tangible nervousness.

It was too quiet.

Carefully, they crept along, keeping close to the wall to ensure they didn't bump into anyone. As they neared the first office, they could see that a person was lying on the ground in the doorway. A pale hand was resting on the ground and the rest of the body was hidden by a white wall.

Rosa backed up, not wanting to go any closer.

Bryan, sensing her fear, whispered, "Stay here. I'll go take a look. If you see anything weird...run back the way we came."

She nodded her head in agreement and stood terrified in place.

Bryan took a deep breath and slowly advanced, each step painfully loud in the silent hallway. As he neared the hand, he could see that the fingertips were stained with blood. In one quick motion, he swung around and looked inside. The hand was connected to the body of a nurse who had been attacked. She was lying face down, but blood seeped out from underneath her body and was spreading. Her left leg appeared to have been pulled out of its socket and was lying at an impossible angle, the foot exposed and missing several toes. Taking a deep breath, Bryan turned the woman over and stared in disbelief.

She had been mauled. Her face was nearly unrecognizable, destroyed by its attacker. Both eyes were missing, the eye sockets torn and bleeding. Long scratches ran down her face in jagged lines and her neck had a large weeping gash that was dripping down and depositing crimson drops into a small puddle on the floor.

Her office was a disaster. All of the hardware had been knocked off the table and bloody fingerprints stained the phone, desk, and wall. Amidst the mess, Bryan noticed that the fax machine had been torn free from the wall and thrown against the floor, but a piece of paper was still lodged inside.

Picking up the machine, Bryan was able to gently extract the paper without tearing it and looked at what had been its last communication.

FAX TRANSMISSION
TO: Nurse May Westin
FROM: Zyne Laboratories, Corp. Office
Urgent Response Requested
Attention Nurse Westin – More test mice are showing signs of severe agitation and muscular reformation. We need to consider a trial termination. Please have Dr. Johns contact me as soon as you can. In the meantime, we've scheduled a meeting with the Executive Committee to discuss our findings and assess the risk of termination.

It is important to ensure that the test subjects are isolated,

Error - Fax transmission terminated due to loss of data receipt

Bryan folded up the fax and put it in his pocket. His mind raced with countless questions and anger boiled inside his chest, but he knew that this was no time to succumb to rage. There were strange sounds coming from the hallway and with Rosa holding down the fort outside, he needed to finish looking around.

Emerging from the room, careful not to step on the dead nurse, he looked back. To his relief, Rosa was still standing there, and was clearly terrified. She nodded her head quickly as he motioned toward the furthest end of the hallway. There were several other open doorways that needed to be explored, so he grabbed a large pair of scissors off a nearby table.

Just in case I need a weapon, he thought.

The hallway was empty and foreboding. Lights continued to flicker on and off and Bryan could hear a soft shuffling sound in the distance. Looking back at Rosa, he knew that there was no choice but to proceed—even with potential danger ahead. He couldn't put her and the others in danger. If Rick threatened him, he would need to handle the man carefully, but Bryan wasn't afraid to defend himself if necessary.

This wasn't Bryan's first time in a potentially violent situation. Growing up in Overtown, Florida, he'd been exposed to tough neighborhoods and rough situations, and knew how to maneuver himself carefully.

He was the first member of his immediate family to successfully finish high school and graduate from college. The NBA had wanted him before he'd received his Bachelor of Science degree from Florida State University, but instead of going pro immediately, he'd held his ground and finished up.

His father's reaction to those choices hadn't been a surprise.

"You're giving up the chance of a lifetime, boy. Don't be stupid. Take it and run. I didn't raise you to be an idiot and make bad ass decisions."

Bryan hadn't even responded. It was easier to hang up the phone, than get into an argument. And he'd still gotten into the NBA. But he often wondered if his family really loved him or the money he sent them every month. Sometimes he felt like a cash cow and once the milk ran out, he'd never hear from them again.

Bryan crept along expertly, watching with keen eyes—preparing to react quickly if something or someone jumped out at him.

Approaching the first office, he quickly determined that it was a laboratory that had been ransacked. The vials housed along the various shelves had been smashed and a strange sulfuric stench filled the air. Gagging, Bryan started to back away but noticed that there were wet footprints on the floor, leading to a large mahogany bookshelf that was separated from the wall with a space behind it that could easily conceal a smaller person. Carefully, he moved toward the bookshelf, preparing himself for the worst.

"Umm, is anyone there?"

No answer.

Feeling ridiculous and frightened at the same time, he crept closer. Now, he could hear a very low sizzling sound. Like bacon frying in a pool of vegetable oil…

Heart pounding, Bryan walked in front of the bookshelf and began to move around to the side. Suddenly a hand shot out and gripped his shirt. As he backed away, the technician who had been hiding came into view.

He was an awful sight. Half of his face had been eaten away as if his attacker had thrown a vial of corrosive solution all over him. Skin was missing, replaced by pink wet ropes. Muscles and the blank white appearance of skull-bone glinted against the synthetic fluorescent lights. One eye was destroyed, a red oozing mess. The other one was swollen and pained as he begged Bryan, "Please help me…"

Bryan gagged and tried not to vomit. Backing away further, he tried to get some information. "What happened to you? Who did this?"

"Not sure…one minute I was…working…next minute, there was acid all over my face. He was crazy…and not…not normal," the man was babbling, barely coherent. He swayed back and forth in place.

"What do you mean, not normal?" Bryan asked, a chill racing through his veins.

"His face…his face was moving. He was like a creature…but a man at the same time…it hurts! You've gotta help me…" and then the technician fell to the floor, shuddering, and fainting in a pain induced coma.

Like a creature? This is totally fucked up, thought Bryan. He backed up again and nearly screamed when a hand reached out and touched his shoulder.

"Damn Bryan, it's just me. Oh shit!" screamed Rosa as the damaged technician came into view.

"I didn't want to wait there anymore. It was totally freaking me out. What the hell happened to him?" she asked.

As quickly as he could, Bryan explained what he'd seen and pulled the wrinkled fax out of his pocket.

After reading the fax, Rosa sighed loudly and decided that it was time to tell him exactly who she was.

When she was done, he was staring at her distrustfully. "So, you knew all along that this clinical trial had problems? Why did you let us all get stuck and fucked with? We're all screwed, aren't we?"

Rosa felt horrible, but knew that she didn't have time to stand and argue. Things were going downhill…fast.

"Look, I need to get my cell phone. If we can call out, then I can reach the CDC and warn them. They'll bring help. We should try to get out of here as soon as possible. I mean, we haven't even tried the front doors yet."

Bryan wasn't sure he wanted to listen to her. After all, she'd been lying for days about being a doctor. But, he had no other choice. He knew that if he didn't at least give her a chance, he could end up like the horrible, messed up bastard lying on the floor.

"Ok. Let's get your phone. Don't fuck with me. We need to grab our shit and get out of here. Do you understand?"

Rosa nodded. "Yes, we need to get out of here, but we've got to take everyone with us."

Suddenly, they heard someone *howling* in the distance. It was a terrifying sound—filled with pain and anguish. Something about it was not quite human and the sound pierced through Bryan and Rosa's bald heads, making their dull headaches even worse.

"What...what was that?" Rosa asked.

"Look, I'm not exactly sure what we're dealing with here, so stay close to me."

The two crept slowly to the doorway and peeked out, just in time to see what looked like Rick stumble to the doors, throw them open, and race out. But just the sight from behind was enough for both of them to realize that there was something seriously wrong with him.

His head was misshapen and bald—all of the new hair, gone. There were large cyst-like lesions protruding from the skull and pushing against the skin. He was also hunched over as if something had happened to his spine. Purplish ooze leaked out of one of his ears and trickled down his neck.

Then, the doors swung shut.

Quickly, Bryan and Rosa checked the other rooms to be sure no one was in immediate danger, and were greeted by dead bodies that had been severely mauled amidst toppled furniture and damaged equipment. The center was in shambles.

Unable to find anyone else, they headed back out toward the hallway.

Forgotten and sitting alone in the common area, trying to read a magazine, Jennifer was tired, feeling like shit, and couldn't believe she had put herself through this torture just to become a redhead. Right now, she was bald, ugly, and left to fend for herself.

Tears welled up in the corners of her eyes.

It isn't fair, she thought. *People always let me down. They think my life's so perfect because I'm rich. But what they don't know is that I'm so unbelievably lonely. And here I am once again…alone.*

Her self-pitying thoughts were suddenly interrupted by a strange, howling sound. She sat straight up and listened.

Silence.

Then, a few moments later, a *crash* as the doors to the clinic banged hard into the walls.

Jumping off the couch, she ran from the room, looking for somewhere to hide. The reception area was empty, so she ran behind the front desk and curled up underneath the counter. Heart racing, she could hear sounds in the distance. The shrill, delicate clinking of glass breaking filled the air as tables were overturned and lamps were tossed from their resting places.

Jennifer couldn't believe what was happening.

Is Rick making all of that noise? And where is everyone else?

She remained frozen in place and prayed that whoever was destroying the Illusions building was not going to find her.

Upstairs, Dan and Teresa were insulated from the sounds below and continued to search the sleeping rooms. After covering Tim with a blanket and putting him in one of the rooms for temporary storage, they found a few members of the cleaning staff. The housekeeping personnel had been hired by Zyne and appeared to be ok, despite the commotion. They reluctantly agreed to help carry Tim's body downstairs once a full search could be completed and at Dan's insistence, nervously gathered together in one of the rooms, locking the door behind them.

Teresa was not feeling well. Her infusion injection site was burning painfully. She followed Dan around as he searched, and finally asked him to stop.

"What's wrong?"

"Dr. Johns, I don't feel well. My eyes feel like they're constantly going out of focus, and I've got a really bad headache. Can we rest for a minute?"

"Yes. Why don't you lie down, while I keep looking around? I'll keep searching and will come back to pick you up in about twenty minutes." He left her and went outside. Looking around to make sure he was alone, Dan pulled a cell phone out of his pocket and quickly dialed his contact at Zyne.

The phone was answered on the first ring.

"Johns, what the hell is going on in there? Since your phone call, we've locked down the facility, but now the CDC is on the way and they're telling us we need to tent the entrances and take other serious measures to quarantine all of you."

Dan tried to keep his voice calm. "Look, the situation is definitely not good. We've got one man down and another missing. All of the subjects are sick. Not sure what's going on here. Seems like it may be some sort of cellular reaction. Either the virus we injected to deliver the therapy is causing the subjects severe distress, or there's a problem with the therapy itself. I'm not sure…"

He was cut off by a harsh response. "You're not sure? You're not fucking sure?! We've got people dying in there Johns. And, I can't let you guys out. Not now. You're gonna have to come up with some sort of explanation as to why that guy died. And it can't be because of his infusion. Do you understand me?"

Dan couldn't believe what he was hearing.

"Sir, we can't keep these people in here if they're really sick. We've got to get them medical attention and ensure we taper them off the therapy..."

"Johns, you listen to me. Get all those folks rounded up. Figure out what you're dealing with and then call me back. Until then, I can't help you. Your career and the company are counting on you to do the right thing here. Don't panic. Figure out what the fuck is happening. Then, call me."

Click.

That bastard just hung up on me, he thought.

Rubbing his eyes and taking a deep breath, Dan returned to check on Teresa. She was lying on the bed asleep. But she looked bad. Her scalp was red and blotchy, the rest of her skin pale.

Sitting on the edge of the bed, Dan thought about Trichotillomania, the compulsion to pull hair out of the scalp or face. His mother had suffered from the same thing and it had frightened him all of his life. She'd been a beautiful woman in her twenties and thirties but her marriage to his father, a well-known local surgeon, had been stressful. Dinner parties, social gatherings—it was all too much for her. She was frail, nervous, and constantly questioning her self-worth. Oftentimes, Dan would observe her sitting at the dining room table, pulling out long strands of black hair and tossing them to the floor. Once, she'd even put one of the strands in her mouth and chewed on it, while looking out in the distance.

This continued throughout his childhood and as the stress increased in his parent's marriage, his mother's tendency got worse. She began regularly pulling out clumps of her hair and started wearing wigs to cover up the self-inflicted baldness.

As the marriage completely disintegrated, she withdrew from society and spent hours in her bedroom, staring at the mirror, pulling out her hair. She also began to pull out her eyebrows and eyelashes. The compulsion became severe and his father finally left, unable to handle her worsening condition.

After the divorce was final, Dan went to live with his father, but returned several weeks later to visit his mother in her new home.

He used the spare key she'd given him to unlock the front door. When he stepped inside, he had to squint to find his way through the entranceway. The house was dark and stuffy as if the air conditioning had been off for several days. The kitchen looked bare, the cupboard devoid of food, the refrigerator containing a carton of milk, ancillary rotting vegetables, and a loaf of moldy bread. Dishes sat in the sink, unwashed, and houseflies buzzed throughout.

"Mom?" he called out. When she didn't answer, he walked to her bedroom and knocked on the door.

A tiny, weak voice shouted out, "Come in."

Dan remembered how frightened he'd been to enter her bedroom. By that point, his mother had become reclusive and strange; her compulsion transforming what was once beautiful into a freakish visage of pain and psychosis.

Slowly pushing the door open, he'd found her sitting at the familiar vanity mirror. Even from his vantage point, he could see patches of bald spots along the back of her head like polka dots. She wasn't wearing a wig and was applying eyebrow pencil to her face.

"Oh, hi my darling…" When she turned to face him, he'd almost screamed, but managed to hold it together through sheer willpower.

She looked like a demented circus clown. No eyebrows remained and were replaced with jagged, misshapen, thick lines. Her hair was thin and missing in many spots, her face gaunt, and her eyes sunken into deep, black crevices. Her skin was thin and stretched, and to make matters worse...she'd applied bright red lipstick, uneven and smudged.

She rose to give him a hug and he couldn't stand it a moment longer. Backing out of the room, he'd raced out of the house, hearing her voice call to him as he'd rushed out...

"Dannnyy...Dannnyyy...come backkk...come backkk...."

That was the last time he saw his mother because a few days later, she committed suicide by swallowing an entire vial of Valium. Her appearance had been so damaged that the funeral parlor was unable to make her presentable. The family decided against a showing and instead, kept her wasted and destroyed frame inside a beautifully adorned coffin, so that the only memories of her would be regal.

But Dan's memories would forever be shattered by his last encounter, and he often revisited their last meeting during nightmares that occurred again and again over the course of his adult life.

Now, sitting on the bed and watching Teresa sleep, he wondered if maybe he'd taken this assignment because of the psychological damage done by his mother. Had he pushed ahead with the trial even though he hadn't been completely sure that it was safe because he was trying to undo the wrongs of his past? To save people who suffered like her? People like Teresa?

Shaking his head, he pushed the questioning thoughts out of his head. These people counted on him to figure out what was going on. He made a silent pact with himself that no matter what, he was going to make things right and help them get better.

Standing up, he decided to let Teresa rest and left her lying on the bed.

Rosa and Bryan were stunned to see the damage done to the common area. Sofas were overturned, the TV was smashed, and glass littered the floor in every direction. Both were careful to not step on any shards and maneuvered over to the dining area without getting hurt.

Bryan wasn't feeling good. His head was pounding and at times it was difficult to put thoughts together. Sneaking a peek over at Rosa, he wondered if she was feeling bad too. The unspoken question hung in the air between them.

Would they both turn into...something psychotic...something like Rick?

They'd both taken the same infusion as Rick and those genes were running through their veins. How long would it take before they were both—sick?

The idea was terrifying and too painful to focus on so they both concentrated on getting Rosa's phone. But crossing over into the reception area wasn't as easy as it seemed. Both were acutely aware that Rick was on the loose and they couldn't simply casually saunter in and grab her cell.

"Look," Rosa said, "I know we need to get in there. I'm not even sure where they put our phones, so we're going to have to search around. We need to move carefully. Let's go get something that we can use as a weapon, because we really don't know what we'll find."

The dining room staff had been on break prior to the official lockdown so the pantry and cooking areas were vacant, giving them free reign to seize the sharpest, longest knives they could find before heading out. The two grabbed several and gripped their weapons tightly, quietly creeping toward the entranceway.

From their hidden vantage point, they could see that the front glass doors were now covered with a yellow tent-like material. Rosa gasped. The CDC or some other high-ranking governmental agency had sealed off the perimeter. She wouldn't be surprised if they found all the other exits sealed and the windows guarded by the military. From her experience, she knew that these types of measures were taken when there was an extreme danger to the public and she wondered if the therapy they'd received not only changed their hair color but also fundamentally altered their cellular structure, making them harmful or contagious.

She and Bryan crept along the wall and finally found themselves standing at the reception area. A sound under the table alerted them that they were not alone.

"Who's there?" shouted Bryan. "Come out, or we'll have to shoot!"

Neither of them had a gun, but he wasn't taking any chances...

Slowly, Jennifer rose from her hiding place and, recognizing them, ran over and hugged Bryan tightly. Tears streamed down her cheeks and she sobbed into his neck.

When she finally calmed down, the three stood close together as she recounted recent events, describing the tornado that had erupted when Rick flew through the common area, destroying everything in sight. She hadn't seen him, but the sounds he'd made were terrifying enough. She'd sat still under the counter for several minutes waiting to see if he would come in and find her, but thankfully, he'd lumbered away in a different direction and disappeared.

"What's wrong with him?" she asked fearfully. "Is the same thing going to happen to us? Oh my God!"

Rosa tried to calm her down. "We don't know what's wrong, so we should stick together and see if we can call for help. It looks like the building is sealed off, so let's see if the doors will open up."

The group tried to open the glass doors and found them locked. Bryan unsuccessfully hurled a chair at the glass, which didn't leave a mark. They quickly realized that they would need to seek another escape route.

"Let's see if we can find those phones," Bryan suggested, "At least before Rick comes back."

They discovered a door along the wall behind the reception area. It was unlocked and led to an office with a phone, fax machine, computer, and several mail slots lining the walls. The three searched the room but could not find their belongings.

Rosa picked up the phone on the desk, hoping to connect through a landline.

It was dead.

Frustrated she sighed and sat down in a chair.

While the other two continued searching, she began to feel a bit of panic rising in her chest. When phone lines were down that could only mean one thing. The entire building was under quarantine. She had worked at the CDC long enough to know when a situation warranted shutting off all communication to the outside world. And that knowledge made her very nervous. She wasn't feeling well, nor were the others. And there was only one person who could help them.

Dr. Dan Johns.

She wondered where he was. He'd gone upstairs with Tim and Teresa a while ago and since then, they hadn't heard from him. She concluded that he was the only person completely clear on what venomous solution was running through their veins and how to fix it.

A sharp pang of pain raced through her skull and for a moment she thought she was going to pass out. Dropping her head between her knees, she moaned, waiting for the sensation to dissipate.

Bryan came over and put his hand on her shoulder. "Are you ok?" he asked.

"Yeah, just not feeling so hot, and I've got this wicked headache."

Bryan agreed. "I'm feeling pretty shitty too. And my eyes are really hurting. Do they look ok to you?"

Rosa peered into one of his eyes and saw a red hue in the iris. The rest of the eye was red-rimmed and appeared inflamed or infected. She hadn't noticed it before because they were too preoccupied with the chaos erupting around them.

"Well?" he asked.

"Your eyes do look a little red, but not too bad," she lied.

Jennifer, who had been searching around in a desk, slammed the drawer and leaned up against the wall. "This is ridiculous. Where they hell did they put our stuff? I swear, I'm going to sue the hell out of these people when we get out of here."

Rosa glared at her and realized that the snooty socialite had no idea just how bad things were. They hadn't shared much with her other than they found Rick running around like a crazy person, and they needed to call for help.

Judging by the way she reacts to things, it's probably for the best, thought Rosa.

After ten more minutes of searching, they agreed that their phones had been hidden somewhere else. In the distance, they heard a voice calling for them.

———

"Bryan...Jennifer...Rosa...where are you guys?" Dan called. He stopped once he got to the common area. The room was an absolute mess. Everything was thrown around or broken. And it wasn't a great mystery as to who had caused all of the destruction.

Unless someone else had…turned…

Dan swallowed hard.

This whole situation is turning into one huge fucking mess, and I don't have much time to come up with a solution.

First he needed to find everyone. He'd left Teresa sleeping upstairs and figured she was safe in her room. After all, the entire cleaning crew was up there with her and could help out if Rick somehow reappeared.

He also decided that it would be best to keep the whole situation with Tim quiet for now. If he shared that the surfer was dead, he could have full-blown hysteria on his hands. Plus, he wasn't sure what condition the subjects would be in. The metamorphosis that was happening within their cells apparently unfolded at a different rate, depending on the person. So, he'd have to be careful.

He found the group sitting in the Illusions reception office. They didn't look good. Bryan, the basketball player, was displaying moderate symptoms and both Rosa and Jennifer seemed sick. He wasn't sure if he was seeing things or not, but Bryan and Rosa's shaved heads appeared slightly swollen.

"Hey guys, how are things down here?" he asked, trying to sound casual.

Bryan actually *growled* at him in anger and was about to say something, when Jennifer cut in impatiently. "What the hell is going on? Why is Rick acting all crazy? When can we get out of here?" Her voice had taken on a shrill edge, and she was clearly a few minutes shy of complete hysteria.

Dan tried to calm her down, "Ok, here's what I think. There's something slightly wrong with the infusion we gave you…"

48

Bryan exploded. "Slightly wrong?! Slightly? Are you out of your fucking mind? Rick is running around like a maniac and there's something wrong with him. He's...he's...an animal. What did you do to us?"

Dan couldn't speak.

They knew...

They knew what they could become. They knew what their fate could be.

He realized that he had no choice, but to tell them about what he'd experienced upstairs. As he found his voice, he carefully recapped recent events and watched as the subjects grew more horrified by the minute.

"Crap. Guys, I'm sorry about this. As you can imagine, we're going to fix this issue. I've just got to get into the lab and work on slightly altering your concoction by lowering the amount of virus we use...it should only take a..."

"Have you seen the laboratory?" Bryan hissed. "It's a disaster area. You'll be lucky to find anything in that mess."

Dan rushed out of the room and down the hallway into the medical center. When he pushed the doors open, his breath caught in his lungs.

Oh no, he thought. *This is horrible! It's gonna take me hours to fix this. And I'm gonna need reinforcements.*

As calmly as he could, he returned to the group. They hadn't moved, just stared at him suspiciously.

"Ok. We've got to find Rick and restrain him. Then, I'll put together an infusion that will help you at least stabilize until we can get some help."

"Yes," said Rosa coldly. "Where is our help? The nurses are all dead, and we can't find our cell phones anywhere. As you know doctor, I'm connected to the CDC and we know that the phones are shut off and the doors are all locked. The building is sealed and covered with a tarp! Why don't you just tell us the truth?"

Jennifer gaped. "You're with the CDC? What the hell?"

Dan turned away and took a deep breath. He hadn't realized that the entire building was now physically sealed off. Trying to regain his composure, he spoke slowly, "Look. I'm telling you the truth. We need to get the whole situation under control and then we'll all be able to get out of here. We need to find Rick first. He's a danger to himself and everyone else."

Teresa awoke slowly and wasn't sure where she was initially. Her surroundings were unfamiliar and it took a few minutes for her to remember that she was napping in one of the rooms within the Illusions building. She blinked slowly and was acutely aware that her whole body felt awful and sluggish. Suddenly, there was a sound emanating from the right side of the room that sounded like grunting. Whatever was near her was panting and very close.

Turning her head slowly, she came face-to-face with Rick, the billionaire she had once known. But the creature that stared back at her was no longer human. And Teresa knew with utmost certainty that she was staring into the face of hell itself.

Rick's entire face had shifted apart, the gray fissure that separated each side much larger now and oozing right down the middle like a swollen river. It began at the base of his forehead and extended downward, splitting his lips in half, so that blood dripped from the crack into his mouth. Each eye was slanted and hazy. She could see that he was in intense pain as the transformation of his skull was literally ripping his face in half. For a moment, their eyes met and Teresa could almost sense that Rick recognized her and was reaching out for help.

But almost as quickly as it appeared, it evaporated and all that remained was a tumultuous mess of what had once been a human being.

It snarled and lunged for her, but Teresa was already rolling off the bed, aiming for the door. Screaming loudly, she raced for the exit, but the creature was close behind, grabbing at her shirt and pulling her back.

Down the hall, the cleaning crew that was waiting in a single locked room heard the commotion and did not move. They all sat still, terrified at what was unfolding several doors down. As Teresa's screams intensified, a member of the group rose to help, but was pushed back down by a larger man.

"Don't go out there, Greg," he warned. You do, and you'll get us all killed. You sit right there and wait for Dr. Johns to come back."

Greg sat back down on the bed, the sounds of violence and death traveling through the air.

Then...all was silent.

CHAPTER 5

D an was worried about Jennifer.
　　She and the others had agreed to help him search for
Rick, but as he walked behind her, he could see sores on the
back of her neck as well as stretch marks on the skin that
covered her skull.

Jennifer couldn't see this because it would require a very
strategically positioned mirror, but Dan could clearly identify
the marks through the bright red stubble of her new hair. This
could only mean one thing.

Whatever happened to Rick, was happening to her. The
metamorphosis had begun.

He wanted to scream in frustration. This was not
happening. How had the infusion gone so wrong?

Logically, Dan knew time was running out and he would
need to work on a solution to counteract the mutation, but with
the medical center in disarray, it would be difficult. He needed
to reach out to Zyne and get reinforcements or the entire mess
would be impossible to clean up.

Excusing himself from the group for a moment, he went into one of the private bathrooms and shut the door. Pulling the cell phone out of his pocket, he quickly dialed Zyne.

"Yes?" A voice answered on the first ring.

"It's Johns. Things aren't going well."

"What do you mean? Have you secured all the subjects?"

"Well," Dan hesitated, "Not exactly. We've still got one missing. Look, the infusion is not working and it's creating a metamorphosis of some sort."

"A metamorphosis? What exactly do you mean, Dr. Johns?"

"Well," Dan said painfully, "The infusion is causing cellular abnormalities at an incredible rate in some of the subjects. It's causing muscular and skeletal deformities, confusion, and…aggression. I need help here."

Silence followed and then, "What kind of help?"

Dan explained how the medical center had been ransacked, with most of the vials destroyed and technicians killed.

"Why has the building been sealed off? Isn't that a little extreme?"

The Zyne representative sounded aggravated and impatient, but explained the need for utmost security.

"We don't want helicopters flying around, taking video of the subjects inside. This way, we can keep their appearance and the whole situation concealed until we're able to take them out and get them to safety. We've just got to handle this carefully…"

Suddenly, the line filled with static and the call dropped. Dan tried to call back several times, but a busy signal rang in his ear.

He would need to try to call again at a later time. The group was probably already wondering what was taking him so long.

Putting the phone in his pocket, Dan wondered where these directives were coming from. Zyne? Government officials? Investors? He didn't want to panic but was slowly realizing that he was trapped as well and wouldn't be let out until he pulled it together.

And that wasn't going to be easy.

Flushing the toilet, he exited the bathroom, only to find Bryan and Rosa standing over Jennifer. She was lying on the ground, eyes shut—a small amount of drool escaping the left side of her mouth.

Dan rushed over to her and listened closely. She was still breathing, which was a good sign. "What happened?"

Rosa responded, "We're not sure. One minute she was standing here with us waiting for you, and the next minute she dropped to the floor."

With Bryan's help, Dan carried her to the couch, laying her down gently.

"Oh my goodness...look!" Rosa gasped.

Jennifer's face was turning red and as her skin cracked, tiny bloody fissures appeared where the skin was beginning to break open. Dan peered closely and could almost see the dermis breaking apart. Underneath, there was slight but noticeable movement as her muscles shifted and her skull changed. It was impossible, but still it was happening...right in front of their eyes.

Bryan suddenly grabbed Dan's shoulders and pushed him up against the wall. Bringing his face within inches, he spat into the doctor's face. "Look, we've been patient enough. Get us the fuck out of here."

Dan was frightened by the athlete's anger, yet understood where it was coming from. They were all frightened—and with good reason.

"Look," he said quietly, "I can't get you out of here until we find Rick and I'm able to inject you with an infusion that will normalize your cells. I'm trapped in here too, just like you guys."

Bryan stepped back in disbelief. "So, you're stuck too? There's no way out? They can't keep us prisoners in here..."

"Unfortunately, they can," Dan said, "It was in the contract you all signed. Basically, your lawyers agreed to leave you in Zyne's custody until we could assure that you were healthy and able to rejoin society with your new full head of hair." He chuckled sarcastically, "This was not part of the plan, believe me. We're sealed off and they've shut down all phone service and communication with the outside world."

"Wait..." Rosa exclaimed, "Where are the cell phones we brought? Can we at least try to call out?"

Dan sighed. "Your phones were taken off property as a precaution. The Zyne Corporation required that we essentially cut you off from the outside world in order to protect the confidentiality and integrity of the study."

"Some integrity..." huffed Bryan, but he was already backing off—defeated and frightened.

The group decided that it would be best to search the second floor of the building together. They hadn't seen Rick anywhere in the vicinity and given all the noise they were making, assumed that he would have made his presence known if he was down there with them.

With all of the medical staff now either dead, injured, or missing, they would have to leave Jennifer alone for the time being. As a precaution, Dan injected her with a mild sedative to keep her calm, though he wasn't sure if it would do much good. After seeing the surfer turn into a lunatic within a matter of minutes, he figured anything was possible.

In preparation for the search, both Bryan and Dan armed themselves with long kitchen knives. The doctor excused himself for a moment and rushed into his office, grabbing a small pistol he kept hidden for emergencies. When Bryan saw the firearm, he grunted in agreement.

The three piled into the elevator and remained silent as the car whooshed and groaned, lifting them to the second floor. Dan felt compelled to provide encouragement though he knew it probably wouldn't do any good.

"Guys, I promise you, I'll do whatever I can to ensure no one else dies today. And if we survive this..."

"If we survive this, we are suing the hell out of the Zyne Corporation as well as you doctor," Bryan finished coldly, looking in the other direction.

That ended the conversation and when the doors opened to the second floor, they all felt the electricity and strangeness in the air. Adding to the gloomy atmosphere was a yellowish glow that filled the hallway due to the fact that the few windows lining the walls were now covered with yellow tarp.

They stepped out of the elevator and stood for a moment as the doors slid shut. Silence surrounded them—a tense silence—and a strange coppery smell managed to find its way to their nostrils.

Dan recognized it immediately.

It was the smell of blood.

Suddenly, they heard a distant snarl coming from down the hall. Rosa instinctively backed up, terrified of what they might find. In all of her years working for the government, she had never experienced anything like this. In the past, she had dealt with sickness, contagion, and even madness. But nothing like this. In training, she'd heard about similar situations and the end result was containment—no matter what it took. The government was unsympathetic and unwilling to save a few sick souls if it meant protecting the masses.

They were all sick—all except for the doctor. And she didn't trust him one bit.

After all, he's the reason we're in this predicament.

Dan and Bryan decided to investigate and left Rosa by the elevators so that she could make a quick getaway if needed.

Together they crept along slowly, passing closed doors and rooms where they'd slept earlier in the week. Up ahead, Dan could see that the door to the room Teresa had been sleeping in—was open.

His heart rate increased. *Damn it,* he thought. *Can't any of these people stay still? It's impossible to get my arms around this when people keep disappearing.*

Only, he wasn't sure if Teresa had disappeared.

As they peered inside, they both gasped instantaneously. Blood was everywhere. On the walls, on the bed, on the carpet...it was smeared on the TV monitor and along the walls. But no sign of Teresa.

"Maybe we should check the bathroom," Bryan whispered.

As they got closer to the bathroom, the smell of blood grew stronger. Dan pulled out the pistol and pointed it straight ahead, prepared to shoot if anyone or anything jumped out at him.

"Hello?" he called out.

Silence.

The two men looked at each other and counted in silence...one, two, three...

They both leapt into the doorway and almost immediately staggered back. Bryan turned away and vomited on the carpet—gagging and choking. But Dan stood in shock, drinking in the horror that now greeted them.

Teresa had been *eaten*.

Her body lay on the floor, flesh torn off her bones in numerous places. Stringy muscle hung in ropes around her arms and legs. What had once been her torso was a gaping red mass. Half-eaten organs lay in disarray on the tile floor. Dan could even identify her heart, a lumpy mess near the toilet bowl.

But the worst part was that Teresa had been decapitated. Her bald, stubbly head was lying in the bathtub, eyes still open. The milky orbs gazed out into nothingness.

Dan couldn't look at the scene any longer. He backed up and stumbled against the blood-splattered bed. Bryan was still gagging and had stepped outside, unable to stand it. Dan followed him out and leaned up against the wall.

Neither man could speak.

Rosa called out to them, "Hey guys...what did you see?"

When they didn't answer, she started to approach them, but Bryan waved her away.

"Don't come over here. It's not good. Oh my God, it's really not good." Bryan slid down and sat on the ground, putting his head between his knees.

"Rosa, just wait for us. You don't want to see this. Teresa...Teresa is dead..." Dan choked and looked away. Things were spiraling out of control. He needed to diffuse the infusion immediately and treat his subjects before he lost everyone. Not caring anymore, he pulled out his cell phone and dialed the laboratory at Zyne.

This time, the phone rang and to his relief, April answered.

"April, it's Dr. Johns."

"Dr. Johns," she whispered. "What the hell is going on? We've got government officials crawling all over the laboratory and they've quarantined Illusions. It's all over the news."

Dan tried to calm her. "April...please calm down. I need your help. Something is wrong with the infusion. It's giving the subjects new hair color, but it's also altering their DNA."

"I know," she responded quickly. "We've been trying to reach you, but haven't been able to get through. All of the mice are...well, they're dead."

He sighed and looked over at Bryan and Rosa who were now both glaring at him as he spoke on the cell.

"I don't have much time. Please, tell me...where are the treatments to stabilize the cells? We need to stop the gene therapy now. And I've got to get these people treated before this gets any worse."

There was noise on the other end as if a door had been thrown open. April whispered, "They've found me talking to you...we're supposed to let them know if you contact me. The solution is in Lab A in the Illusions building...just look for the vial marked...hey! Give me back my phone!"

Click.

Dan stared at the dead phone in his hand.

Poor April, he thought. He had worked with her for many years, having trained and then partnered with her on different projects. She was kind and attractive, with an extremely sharp mind. They'd had a few beers and spent time together away from the laboratory, becoming good friends. Dan knew that April was a genuine person and tried to mentor her as best as possible on how to be successful not only in the laboratory, but also in life. She often sat and listened to him, with her big brown eyes soaking up his words of wisdom. It made him feel important and sometimes he wondered if perhaps he had a bit of a crush on her. Knowing that she was in trouble made his stomach lurch and the world suddenly swayed in front of his eyes in a sea of wobbling uncertainty.

"So, no cell phones in the building, huh?" asked Bryan accusingly.

Before Dan could say anything, Bryan snatched the phone out of his hand and pushed him up against the wall. Dan felt the cool concrete pressing against his back and tried to look away.

"Well? Care to answer me doc?" Bryan asked menacingly.

"Look, I was going to tell you, but..." Suddenly Bryan elbowed Dan in the gut, knocking all of the air out of him. He moved away and dialed 911, but instead of the phone ringing, all he heard was a busy signal on the other line. He tried over and over but got the same result.

Throwing the phone on the floor, he turned to Rosa, ignoring Dan who was now on the floor wincing in pain.

"I'm going to look for a way out. We can't trust him. He's been lying the whole time. Are you coming with me?"

Rosa stared at the doctor who was still bent over in pain. She was furious with him as well. If he'd just told them about his cell phone, maybe she could have called someone and explained the situation properly. But now, they were stuck and with no way out and no quick solution, their bodies were taking over and fast becoming something else.

Their cells were changing.

She could feel it. Her head was hurting constantly now and periodically, her vision would blur. It also felt at times like there were little bugs crawling underneath her skin and she found herself scratching her arms and legs. She noticed that Bryan was doing the same thing.

Maybe it's a good thing that we're quarantined. Who knows what we'll turn into, she thought.

"Ok. Let's go. But Bryan..."

"Yes?"

"If we can't find a way out, we're going to need him." She pointed in Dan's direction. "He's the only one here who can treat us and possibly reverse the damage."

Bryan snorted in annoyance. "Yeah, ok. But let's leave him for now. I can't stand looking at that asshole."

Dan mumbled in pain, "We...we...need to stay together."

"Fuck you," Bryan retorted, "You lied to us. And you may have killed us. So just stay the hell away."

"Dr. Johns, we're going to look for a way out. We'll come back for you later." And with that, Rosa nudged Bryan and the two rang for the elevator.

Once it arrived, they got in and watched as the doctor sat on the floor, and put his head up against the wall. He didn't try to follow them and remained in place as the elevator doors closed.

As they descended to the first floor, Rosa took Bryan's hands in hers. She felt bad for the athlete, who seemed so dejected. And despite the ailments that were taking over, she was attracted to him. His red-rimmed eyes were gentle and large, giving his face character and revealing wise tendencies. It didn't hurt that he was tall and muscular as well. And feeling this sick had heightened her internal loneliness.

She *needed* to be wanted...

As she held his hands, he stared back at her and felt an attraction as well. He wasn't sure if it was the infusion or just the hopelessness of the situation, but as they stood in close proximity, his loins began to tingle and heat spread throughout his crotch. His penis began to harden and when they stepped out of the elevator, he pulled her to him and gave her a deep kiss.

Rosa couldn't believe what was happening, but couldn't stop herself. Within the scope of a minute, her body had turned into a raging inferno of aching desire and she kissed him back fervently. Her crotch was wet and screaming with desire.

Bryan stepped back from their kiss and lifted her up off the ground. Without saying a word, he picked her up and placed her on the couch Jennifer had been lying on. The socialite was gone, but neither of them cared or noticed. They were both aching and burning with an unnatural lust that was a symptom of their sickness—and needed release from each other.

As slowly as he could bear, he kissed her mouth, neck, and ears. His tongue traveled along the length of her neck and after a few tugs of her blouse, found swollen breasts. Her nipples were dark and erect, shivering as he gently licked each one.

They undressed while at the same time, licking and devouring each other. Once they were both nude, they held each other, sweat intermingling, kisses continuing as their bodies began to melt into each other. They didn't care who saw them or watched—they were hungry with sexual passion heightened by the cellular activity happening deep within their veins.

Rosa grabbed Bryan's erect penis and shoved it deep within her, allowing it to fill and momentarily soothe her aching hunger, but within seconds, the two began to move together in a dance of desire and desperation. They both moaned loudly, their deepening voices sounding more like wolves than humans. They thrust against each other faster and faster, the sexual sweetness of the oncoming release taunting them, forcing them to continue.

As Bryan neared climax, his entire body tightened, and the bones and muscles under his skull pulsed in an unseen oceanic dance. He was glistening with sweat, breathing heavily, and reaching for the pinnacle of their action.

And then, they both came together. Screaming, they writhed and held tight as the sensations flooded their bodies.

As they both stilled and rested, Rosa felt Bryan's head resting on her neck and felt the need to say…something. He was still throbbing inside her, his body warm and wet. Her vision was blocked by his stubbly skull but it was comforting to be surrounded by his essence.

"That was…incredible…" she whispered.

Bryan was silent. She waited for him to say something, and when he didn't, she whispered in his ear, "Bryan, we need to get dressed. Someone might see us. Though, I wouldn't mind doing that again," she chuckled.

Bryan still did not respond and as his penis began to shrink within her, Rosa felt the weight of his body. He felt almost *too* heavy.

Oh my God, she thought.

In the distance, Rosa thought she heard something or someone snarling, but couldn't see anything because of her position. She took Bryan's head in her hands and shifted it so that she could see him.

And then, she screamed.

Bryan's eyes had rolled backwards and only the whites showed. His tongue that had given her such pleasure only moments ago, was now hanging slack out of the side of his mouth.

He was dead. And he was still inside her.

Rosa rolled off the couch on to the floor, taking Bryan with her. His body made a loud thud as it hit the ground. Shrieking, she pushed as hard as she could, shoving his body away and searching for her clothes.

As she quickly dressed, she found herself weeping at the same time. Bryan didn't deserve this. None of them did. And now, the man she'd just had sex with was dead. Unable to stare at his sightless eyes one moment longer, she snatched a blanket off of one of the recliners and gently covered his body.

Just then, Rosa heard snarling in the distance. Suddenly, she remembered that Jennifer had been lying on the couch and was now missing.

"Jennifer?" she called out. Once again, she heard the same strange snarling sound.

Not wanting to be caught off-guard, Rosa grabbed the knife she'd been carrying and headed toward the pool area. She had a strong feeling that the doors would be locked, but decided to give them a try anyway. As she yanked on the handles, the glass doors swung open easily, much to her surprise.

Once outside, it was hard to breathe.

The entire area was covered with a yellow tarp that hung above the ground, fastened to the roof and extending over the pool deck. It was taut and bright, the hot Florida sun seeping through the yellow material. The tarp was creating a greenhouse effect, making the pool area hot and humid. Rosa looked around and could see shadowed shapes in the distance moving about.

Trying to not draw attention to herself, she wiped her tears away, got on the ground and crawled over to one of the poolside tables. Climbing on to the table, she pulled out the knife and began trying to slice open the tarp. It was tough and strong, but she shoved the tip of the knife against it and finally heard a pop as the yellow material snapped open. A sliver of clear blue peeked through, the sky clear and hot. Gasping, Rosa worked on the hole, trying to make it larger when a nearby snarl caught her attention.

Jennifer staggered out into the pool area, snarling and scratching her scalp. Her head was full of bright red sprouts, her eyes wild with pain. She stumbled for a moment as if unsure where to go, but when her eyes connected with Rosa, she screeched and ran forward, arms outstretched. Drool dripped from between her teeth down her neck and soaked into her halter top, which was dark with sweat.

Rosa stood frozen for a moment, unsure what to do. She looked around quickly but it was too late. Jennifer crashed into the table and sent it flying into the pool. The force knocked the knife out of her hand and it dropped on to the deck. In a dizzying splash, Rosa hit her head on the side of the table and fell into the water. Darkness threatened to overtake her mind, but she fought back. Rising to the surface, she gasped and looked around quickly. Jennifer was still standing on the deck, looking at her and grasping at the air as if trying to catch an invisible assailant.

Rosa ducked under the water and swam toward the stairs, trying to get away from the madwoman. She was close to the shallow end, when she felt a hand grab her leg. As she turned around underwater, she could see Jennifer splashing and swimming toward her.

Rosa kicked out and connected with Jennifer's face, managing to free her leg. She came up for air and gasped, just in time for Jennifer to come up behind her and try to grab at her shirt, mouth open... teeth bared. Rosa struggled and pulled away but Jennifer leapt on top of her, dragging her underneath the water.

Underwater, Rosa struggled and pulled Jennifer down too. The women fought each other as the lack of oxygen began to create pressure in both of their chests. Feeling desperation rise in her lungs, Rosa bit down hard on Jennifer's hand, feeling muscles tear as she ripped down and pulled.

It did the trick.

Jennifer let go of her arm, giving her enough momentum to kick out and connect with a knee. That helped to loosen the grip of Jennifer's other arm. Rosa pulled away and rose to the surface, greedily sucking down oxygen. She could feel Jennifer, even in her madness, try to surface and breathe, so she pushed down and held her under the water.

Jennifer thrashed and fought for what seemed like forever. But then the movement slowed, weakened, and finally stopped.

When Rosa stepped away, she watched as one of the nation's most popular socialites floated away and remained submerged underwater while a small cloud of red seeped out from her bitten hand.

Shaking and terrified, Rosa stepped out of the pool and sat down on a lounge chair. Watching the water drip down her head and splatter against the yellow-hued concrete, she could hear people running around outside. Her plan to escape—foiled.

Standing up, she walked toward the hole she'd cut open. Rosa found a chair nearby and dragged it over so that it was positioned directly under the opening. She knew it would be better to draw attention to herself and try to make contact, as opposed to cutting a larger hole and trying to escape. From her experience she knew that there was a chance of getting shot if discovered trying to flee a quarantined zone.

Stepping up on the chair, she shouted out, "Hello...can anyone hear me? It's Rosa Rodriguez with the CDC. I was a test subject, and I've got some information!"

Voices shouted in the distance. She could hear car doors slam and heavy feet trample on concrete. Muffled voices were in discussion and she was about to shout out again when a loud, amplified voice carried over to her. It sounded like it was reverberating through a megaphone.

"Ma'am, please stay where you are. Help is arriving shortly. We need you to remain calm and wait for our instructions."

Rosa was pissed. She knew the drill better than anyone. The mediator on the other side of the tarp was trying to placate her as she'd seen a million times. Normally, she was on the other side – in the real world, while the poor victims being quarantined were getting the same phony bullshit.

She decided to try again.

"Please, we need help immediately. Several people are dead and we need medical supplies to help those of us who are still alive. Please help us. I'm with the CDC."

"Ma'am, we heard you the first time. Please remain calm. Help is on the way."

Rosa tried another tactic. "Dr. Johns asked me to communicate with you. He needs some additional supplies to buffer the transfusion we've received."

This time, another voice responded, "Where is Dr. Johns? Why isn't he talking to us?"

Rosa thought quickly of the best way to respond. "Dr. Johns is in the medical lab. He asked me to come out here and talk with you."

Silence…and then…

"Ma'am, please have Dr. Johns come out here and speak with us. And don't try to further tamper with the protective film you see hanging over the building. If you continue to destroy it, we'll have to take additional measures. It's for your protection and ours."

Rosa wasn't sure what to say. She wanted to shriek and curse at them…calling them every horrible name imaginable. But the more logical side of her brain reminded her that losing her cool would only make the situation worse.

"Got it. I'll bring back Dr. Johns so that you can speak to him directly."

As she stepped off the chair, the world swayed, causing her to fall back and sit for a moment. Her head was pounding in pain and tears formed in the corners of her eyes, spilling down in silent rivers. She heard a helicopter overhead and imagined it hovering over the building in a menacing bug-like manner.

She knew that the CDC had to follow protocol, but couldn't believe that she was being contained in this yellowish prison. Didn't they realize that there were sane people inside who needed help? Yes, most of the nurses and technicians had been killed but there was still one person alive in the laboratory and the cleaning crew was still alive. And…she and Dan were still ok.

Staring at Jennifer's body floating underwater in the pool, Rosa realized that she was now in a life or death situation, and she would need to think rationally and calmly in order to survive. Whatever infusion they'd taken was having a deadly impact and transforming them into wild, sex-crazed, insane animals with little comprehension of right from wrong. She wasn't sure how long she would remain sane—but so far she was able to keep her train of thought steady and wasn't blacking out. Having unprotected and unplanned sex with a stranger wasn't a great way to behave, but she knew her actions could become much worse. The constant itching sensations and headaches were a part of the ongoing transformation.

Rising from the chair, she picked up her knife and decided to head back inside and find the doctor who had started the horrific mess.

Dan watched the elevator doors close and leaned back up against the wall. He didn't blame Bryan and Rosa for being angry. They were starting to realize how bad the situation was getting and needed to blame someone.

That someone was him.

And now, all cell service had been cut off and he was stuck with busted vials and extremely limited supplies. Still, he felt a little better knowing where to find the transfusion buffer.

Thank goodness for April, he thought.

A sound further down the hallway caught his attention. Remembering that the cleaning crew was still cowering in one of the bedrooms, he made his way to their location and knocked on the door.

"Hello? It's Dr. Johns. Please let me in."

He heard a click as the lock turned and the door opened, revealing four very frightened people inside. The men and women were pale and silent, waiting for him to give them some good news.

After he shared with them what was happening, the group decided to stay put. They had water, snacks from a minibar that had been stocked for the study, and a bathroom. Clearly enough to sustain them until the entire ordeal was over. When asked about the yellow material that now covered the windows, Dan lied and said it was all protocol and that they would be allowed to exit the building shortly.

No sense in getting these poor people all freaked out.

While the majority of them appeared to believe him, one man in particular appeared to question what was being shared. He was a shy, quiet sort of person who kept to himself.

Dan asked him his name.

"Greg," the man answered simply and looked away.

Dan didn't have time to try to convince Greg that everything was ok. He needed to search the remainder of the hallway and the storage areas at the far end. Rick was still missing and needed to be restrained...or killed. So, it was necessary to get moving and continue his search.

Standing up to go, he looked back at the small group and apologized to them. "I'm so sorry that you're caught in the middle of this. We'll get it under control and then I'll come back for you." He turned toward the door, when a hand caught his arm.

It was Greg.

"Doctor...can I come with you? I'd sure like to help. It's better than sitting here."

Dan hesitated for a moment and then decided to take Greg up on his offer. He *did* need the help and given Rick's possible strength, it would be good to have back-up.

"Ok, but follow me closely."

As soon as the men left the room and shut the door behind them, Dan pulled Greg aside and whispered, "I don't know if you quite understand what we're dealing with. The man who's missing, Rick, isn't well. In fact, he's lost his mind and could be very dangerous. Are you going to be ok?"

Greg looked at him and nodded. "Yes, we heard. He completely tore up that poor woman while we listened in the other room. I can't just sit and not try to help. And, I don't think you were telling us the truth. We're not getting out of here unless we catch him. Am I right?"

Dan hesitated for a moment and decided that the young man, who appeared to be in his early twenties could be trusted to not panic the group. "Yes, you're right. We're quarantined here until we can treat all of the trial subjects." He looked down the hall. "Luckily, I think I'll be able to treat them, but it's going to be impossible if we can't contain all the subjects who are still alive. We could get ambushed and that would be..."

Suddenly, they heard a roar coming from a storage room that was located at the end of the hallway. Both men could tell that the room had been breached as the door was slightly ajar.

The sounds of boxes being tossed around and metal clanking erupted and sifted towards them. They could also hear someone growling in a deep, inhuman voice. Dan pulled out his gun and grabbed the knife from his belt, handing it to Greg who looked a little uneasy.

"I know it's not much, but you need to be armed."

Greg nodded his head and the two men began creeping toward the storage area. As they moved stealthily, Dan realized that they only had weapons and no way to restrain Rick if they were able to catch him. They would either kill him or he would kill them.

A guaranteed mission failure…

He turned to Greg and motioned to the elevator. "We're making a mistake going down there like this. First, we need to go downstairs and get a sedative. I need to examine Rick to see if I can help him."

The men turned around and quickly made their way to the elevator. After pressing the call button, the doors slid open and they got inside, but just as the doors were closing they saw Rick stumble outside.

Then, the doors shut and they began to descend to the first floor.

"Shit," said Dan, "I hope he doesn't hurt any of the other people up there."

Greg just stared at him frightened and concerned. As the elevator landed on the first floor and the doors once again slid open, Dan thought he heard sounds coming from the common area, but quickly moved in the other direction toward the medical clinic.

Need to get the strong sedatives loaded, he thought.

Motioning for Greg to be quiet, the two men crept along to the clinic. The metal doors were shut and it was quiet inside. Carefully, Dan pushed the doors open and they slowly entered.

Greg's eyes widened and his lips pursed as they passed the dead nurses and the unconscious technician.

Dan noticed Greg's reaction to the technician. "There's nothing we can do for him right now. We've got to leave him here until things are under control."

As they got closer to the last laboratory marked Laboratory A, Dan took a deep breath and said a little prayer to himself. If Rick had destroyed this room, they would be completely out of luck.

He peeked around the corner, gun pointed straight ahead, and was surprised and relieved to see that the laboratory hadn't been completely disrupted. A chair was lying on the floor, but the vials lining the walls were unbroken. And most importantly, the glass casing that he assumed held some of the anti-therapy virus/gene concoctions was unharmed.

Ok, before I do anything, I've got to find the sedatives and load them into a few syringes so that we've at least got a chance.

A built-in sink contained several drawers. He tugged on the first few and pulled out three sterile syringes. Dan then walked over to the glass enclosure and pulled out a mixture that was simply marked "zzz". In preparation for the trial, the technicians had jokingly marked the sedatives with the letters "zzz" to emulate the "zzz's" their patients would experience in the event of an injection.

Dan quickly and expertly filled the syringes with the sedative, careful to not spill any and ensuring that the right amount was extracted. He purposefully filled the syringes with enough liquid to cause a severe blackout in just about any sized person, but not enough to affect the heart or other organs.

Once he was done, he packed the syringes away in a small black case. Looking quickly around the room, he spotted a number of lab coats hanging on the back of the door. He grabbed one and put it on, slipping the casing into a front pocket.

Dan then searched for the vials of the anti-therapy or what the technicians called "buffers". After rifling through the glass enclosure, he finally found what he was looking for.

A row of vials marked "Z-"was neatly hidden behind a row of other vials marked "Z." Dan knew this had been done on purpose. The study had been carefully orchestrated and in order to keep the optimism alive and the technicians on track, the anti-therapy infusions had been hidden.

Yep, we were arrogant and dumb, Dan thought bitterly.

He carefully moved the vials filled with the gene therapy buffer into one of the sturdier wooden cabinets and locked them in with a key he had pulled out of his pocket. It was a skeleton key that was able to unlock every door and cabinet in the Illusions building. After securing the vials, he looked over at Greg and nodded grimly.

"Ok, I think we're ready. Let's go back upstairs."

The emptiness and silence downstairs were disconcerting, but there was no time to worry or do a quick perimeter search. Both men thought about Rick upstairs, potentially doing severe damage and felt anxiety creeping into their minds. They got back in the elevator and pressed 2.

The altercation with Jennifer and interactions with the people keeping them hostage exhausted Rosa and she knew that if she didn't rest for a moment, she wouldn't make it any further. She barely had any energy left to spare, so she decided to lay down on a couch by the front door and take a short nap. Sleep was a sweet escape, but a short time later, different sounds woke her up.

And waking up was *not* a pleasant experience.

Her head felt like it was on fire. Every few minutes, strong pain would shoot through her sinuses and erupt in the center of her skull. It felt as if someone was setting off fireworks in her brain.

This must be what death feels like, she thought.

Suddenly, she felt something dripping down her neck. Reaching up, she touched the liquid and saw that it was crimson. Blood had begun leaking out of her ears. Shaking now, she reached for a nearby box of tissues and quickly dabbed her ears.

She was falling apart.

Don't give up, her inner voice commanded.

Find the doctor…he can help you…

Standing up, Rosa threw the tissues on the table and walked over to the elevator. Each step was painful, but she didn't care. If she stopped now, she had a feeling that she would end up like Jennifer.

Pushing the elevator button, she waited for it to arrive. Once inside and on her way to the second floor, she leaned up against the wall and looked at her reflection in the mirrored walls. She could see that her face was changing.

Her skin was gray and appeared to be stretched. Like Rick, she could actually see her skull separating in half. The stubble on her head stood straight up and reflected the white fluorescent light from overhead. Sometime within the past hour, her nose had started bleeding and there were dried crimson flakes rounding out each nostril. Her eyes were now red-rimmed, and she could see little sores dotting her neck.

She was mutating.

The elevator doors opened and Rosa stepped out. The hallway was empty, but she could hear male voices in the distance and saw that a door was open at the far end. She could vaguely hear someone speaking. Pulling out the knife that she had lodged against her waistband, she held it out in front of her and walked slowly toward the door.

As she got closer, she could hear the commotion.

Dan was shouting in the distance. "Stay right there. Don't move toward him…it's going to make things worse."

Then, she heard a sound unlike anything she'd ever come in contact with before. It was like a wolf baying at the moon.

Whooo….Whooo…

Rosa's heart skipped a beat. *What the hell was that?* she wondered.

Stepping closer to the door, she could now see that a lit bulb hung from the ceiling, casting a dim, yellow glow that permeated the inky darkness. She moved to the doorway, and recognized the space as a large storage room with complicated shelving lining the walls, housing numerous unmarked boxes. All of that however, was inconsequential because it was the center of the large gloomy space that caught and held her attention.

Dan was standing off to the side wearing a white lab coat while another man stood close behind him. Rosa didn't recognize the other man but figured he was with the Illusions staff. Dan had a small syringe pointed at their aggressor who stood only a few yards away.

It was Rick…and he looked like nothing she could have ever imagined. He no longer resembled a human.

His head had changed shape and was now oblong. It had split open at the top and a large wet gap traveled from the top of his head to his chin. It was oozing blood that dripped everywhere, creating a large pool on the ground. One of Rick's eyes had popped out due to the pressure on his skull and was hanging out of the socket. The other eye had burst in the socket and was now a red and white sightless mass. Blood poured out of his nose and his mouth was a grotesque quad-shaped mess of lips, blood, and crimson-stained teeth.

Large sores dotted Rick's skin and oozed grayish matter, giving his exposed arms a wet appearance. He stood in the center of the room, swaying from left to right, as if unsure where to go. He let out another loud moan and Rosa gasped, the sound catching Dan's attention.

The doctor looked over at her and said calmly, "Rosa, don't come any closer. We're going to try to sedate him." And as he said the words, he moved slightly closer. Rick still hadn't moved, but was now swaying more dramatically as if about to break into a strange dance.

Suddenly, the Rick-creature leapt forward, screeching. Dan tried to get out of the way but was pushed to the side and flew into the wall, hitting it...hard.

Rosa backed up. The oozing mess that had once been Rick slowed and was a handful of steps in front of her. Standing this close to him, she could see just how torn his skin appeared. It was stretching apart and had taken on a grayish hue similar to her own. Sloshing sounds emerged from his torn clothing as liquid seeped out of unseen parts of his body, darkening a dirtied collared shirt and dripping in many different directions.

Disgusted and trying not to vomit, Rosa took another step back. She was terrified and unsure where to go. There was nowhere to run...and within seconds she would be torn to pieces. Closing her eyes, she said a small prayer and succumbed to what lie ahead.

As if sensing her defeat, the Rick-creature dove forward, emitting a loud moan. Rosa flinched and prepared herself for a mauling. But it never came.

Slowly opening her eyes, she saw the creature on the ground. Three syringes stuck out of his back.

Dan was on the ground, breathing heavily and sitting on top of Rick, continuing to hold him down as the sick man twitched violently. Then, finally...the twitching stopped and an impossible snore came out of torn nostrils, spewing little droplets of blood during each exhale.

Shaking, Rosa whispered, "Thank you..." and fell to the ground in exhausted tears.

Greg came over and knelt down, gently holding her as she cried.

Getting Rick out of the storage room and into the elevator wasn't easy. After discussing different scenarios, the three agreed that the best way to get him out was to drag him by his feet. So Dan, assisted by Greg, dragged Rick down the hallway. Rosa couldn't bear to touch him and watched as the creature's head vibrated and shifted from side-to-side, leaving a moist path along the carpeted flooring.

Rick was unconscious but still able to moan in pain as if even the darkness of sleep couldn't provide relief from the deadly transformation destroying his body.

Rosa watched and felt anxiety increase her heart rate. She wasn't interested in turning into a maniacal, sick creature and was relieved that at least the doctor was safe and they were heading back down to the laboratory where hopefully she could be cured.

Once the elevator doors opened, they pulled the body inside. Dan sighed with relief as they began to descend once more.

"Ok, we're going to get him into the lab and see if the anti-therapy works. I really wish our friends in the cleaning crew could help out…"

Despite pleading with them, the remaining members of the Illusions facilities team refused to budge. They were all scared, some of them trying to get drunk off the small liquor bottles stocked in the mini-bar. With the exception of Greg, they were content to sit and wait for help to arrive.

If it arrived at all…

As they continued to drag Rick's body to the medical center, Rosa shared that Bryan had died — though she omitted that fact that he died during sex with her and just made it sound like he had collapsed. She then described her altercation with Jennifer. Rosa talked about her ability to breach the yellow tarp-like material that was now covering the building and then recounted her exchange with the people keeping them hostage.

Staring directly at Dan, she shot out, "So, you must know how we can get out of here. Don't even try to deny it. There's gotta be a way."

Dan looked away. "The exits are pretty obvious, Rosa. The problem is they've got us wrapped up in here like sticks of bubblegum. We're not able to get out and we've got to hurry up and get things under control, because I'm sure that our available oxygen is starting to run out."

The group was silent for a moment. Rosa hadn't thought about that. She'd been so concerned about her own metamorphosis that the fact that the building was encased in yellow material finally reached her senses, making her dizzy.

The air *was* getting warm.

Feeling like she was about to pass out, Rosa stopped moving and reached out for the closest wall. Finding one to her right, she put both hands flat against the surface and rested her aching head against it.

The men stopped moving Rick, and both turned back to look at her.

"Rosa, are you ok?" Dan called out. "We can stop and rest for a bit if it would help."

"No," she muttered quietly, "I'm ok. Let's just get moving."

The group moved through the downstairs area as quickly as they could. Again, Dan could not believe how quiet it was. All of the staff was dead...a result of Rick's handiwork. The mangled technician had also died—a gruesome discovery made by Dan and Greg on their way out of the medical clinic.

And the only other people alive were upstairs, cowering in a small room.

Sighing, Dan kept moving despite the muscles in his arms screaming with tension. Greg didn't complain, but he did grunt once or twice when having to turn a corner or reposition Ricks greasy leg under his arm.

Finally, the group made it to the medical clinic. They managed to throw the doors open and carry Rick inside, moving down the hallway. The flickering lights and disarray made their progress seem surreal. At one point, Dan looked back to see Rosa staggering down the hallway, gray and sick. He worried that she would completely transform before they were able to restrain her, but for now, she was manageable.

He was still having trouble accepting that the infusion was a disaster. Try as he might, he couldn't figure out where they had gone so terribly wrong. Had they rushed the trial? Was there something he had overlooked in the research? Many questions tumbled through his mind as the doctor tried to rationally understand how he could have made such a mess of things.

Would they be allowed to leave? And what would face him on the "outside"? Would he be arrested for manslaughter and negligence? Would Zyne Corporation go out of business?

The questions went on and on, but Dan couldn't stop to worry or analyze the potential ruin of his future. Right now, he had to try to cure the two remaining subjects or they would die.

It was that simple.

Getting Rick's body on the makeshift operating table was difficult. His body was engorged with fluids, making his normally stocky frame nearly impossible to lift. He had also become quite slippery; the ooze from his sores leaking out everywhere in a disgusting mess. They all found themselves gagging as they tried to maneuver around the liquid and ignore the acrid stench emitted from the decaying flesh.

Finally, after nearly ten minutes of struggling, they were able to hoist Rick's body into position. It landed with a loud *splat* on the shiny metallic surface. The group immediately restrained him by tying his body down with a series of ropes they'd taken from the storage closet, wrapping it around his legs, arms, and knees.

When Rick was entirely secured, Dan went and quickly filled additional syringes with sedatives. He returned to the room and emptied several syringes into the unconscious man's arm.

"Don't want to take any unnecessary risks," he said, flashing a humorless smile.

He then went and unlocked the cabinet containing the anti-therapy, carefully pulling out the vials. Extracting the bright blue liquid into a clean syringe, he found a vein and injected the infusion into Rick's arm.

"I'm going to try this on Rick first," Dan explained. "Then, we'll know if it's safe to administer to Rosa."

They all stood quietly for a moment, watching the creature sleep in a dark, unconscious haze. Even in this controlled state, the Rick-creature looked awful. His skull continued to pulse as blood leaked from his ears and nose. His useless eye was coagulating in its socket as the chasm separating the two sides of his face continued to glisten and run; a river of disintegrating flesh and sickness.

Suddenly, Rosa fell back as a sharp bolt of pain shot through her skull, traveling down to her toes. She dropped to the ground and watched as a stream of blood flooded her vision, leaking down her nose and into her mouth. Gasping, she looked up at Dan and whispered, "Help me..."

Dan rushed over, and pulled off his lab coat, gently wiping the blood off of her face. The blood was coming from a gash in her forehead that had appeared out of nowhere and was slowly growing in a vertical fashion. He held the fabric close against the wound and pressed down to stop the blood from seeping out, while Rosa clutched his arm and shook against him.

"Why is this happening? What's in the therapy you gave us?" she asked, pleading with him to provide her with some sort of explanation.

"I'm not sure," he replied. "It could be that your cellular structure has been impacted by either the virus we used to transport the genes or it could be the genes themselves. I'm not sure and without the proper instrumentation and time, it'll be impossible for me to figure out."

Rosa was silent. She knew that if the infusion didn't work on Rick...all was lost.

Once the bleeding stopped, Dan was able to leave Rosa's side and check in on his other patient who was still lying on the table, snoring loudly. Blood had pooled under him and ooze continued to seep through and drip past the table on to the floor.

In the doctor's experience, he knew that he had to give the infusion at least several hours before he could do any sort of tests, but he didn't have that type of luxury. So, he found another unused syringe in one of the drawers, and carefully extracted some of Rick's blood. He pulled out the syringe and set it down on the table, preparing to view slides under a powerful SEM microscope to see exactly what was going on with the cells. He pulled up a chair and set it down next to the equipment. When he was positioned properly, he carefully handled the blood, while moving as quickly as possible.

He sat and stared at the specimen under the lens. He could see all sorts of strange activity but wasn't sure exactly what was going on. The red and white blood cells weren't acting normally. If anything, they appeared to be dividing over and over. But as he watched, the cells weren't replicating themselves; rather they were diluted somehow—and seemed like faded replicas of their original state.

Pushing his chair back from the table, Dan ran his hands through his hair. The original infusion was flawed...hence, the anti-therapy was also flawed. It only made sense.

How can you fix something, when you don't know how bad it's going to get? he thought bitterly.

Looking over, he watched as Rosa and Greg stood together against the wall. Rosa's head rested against Greg's chest and she stared out into space, pain reflected in her red eyes. Greg had his head against the wall, his eyes closed, as if saying a private prayer that would save them all.

Dan realized what he had to do. It was an extremely difficult decision for him to make, but there was no choice now.

Pulling the gun out of his pocket, he slowly pointed it at Rosa.

"Rosa, I'm sorry to do this, but I've got to restrain you. Please don't hate me. I've got to do this."

Rosa stared at him in disbelief. Despite her pain, she was still able to hang on to clarity and looked into the barrel of the pistol as it pointed straight at her.

"Why are you doing this?" she asked. "I'm ok...I'm still ok. Can't you fix..." her voice died away when she realized that the answer was now crystal clear. "You can't cure me. I'm sick and there's no way for you to fix me."

"I'm not sure. Initial test results aren't good, but that doesn't mean it won't work. We don't want to make things worse, so I've got to make sure the infusion is safe before giving it to you. It's probably best to restrain you until we can be certain of the outcome."

Greg had not backed away from Rosa and was staring coldly at the doctor. He hadn't said a word in hours, but now looked calm and serious. He stepped between Rosa and Dan. "Put the gun down," he said, "If you don't, you'll have to kill me too and then you'll have more blood on your hands than you can imagine. I'm not going to let you tie her up. She's sick, but she's not a threat. And you," he said pointing at the doctor, "You caused this. You're the reason all these people are dying."

With that, he took Rosa's hand and the two of them walked out of the laboratory. For a moment, Dan considered shooting them both, but realized that Greg was right. If he killed them, he would be arrested for murder, because Greg was healthy and unaffected.

Still, the decision to leave with Rosa worried Dan. She was very sick and changing rapidly. In his expert opinion, Greg was making a potentially deadly decision.

CHAPTER 6

O utside the Illusions building, there were layers of officials,
guards, scientists, and gaping onlookers who had pulled
over to see what all the commotion was about.

The first layer closest to the building consisted of armed
national guardsmen who patrolled back and forth, guns cocked
and ready to fire. They were positioned at every end of the
building, sweating in the Florida sun, and a bit bored. This was
not the most exciting assignment but according to their
superiors...one that required the utmost scrutiny. They hadn't
been fully briefed about what was going on inside, yet they
understood that a clinical trial involving gene therapy and
sponsored by a beauty products giant had gone very wrong and
the general public could be in danger. Immediate containment
had been required and within a few hours of notification, the
group had arrived and commenced quarantine.

Beyond the national guardsmen, small white tents had been
erected and were filled with government officials as well as
representatives from the Zyne Corporation. With grim faces,

reports were filed and updates were given as authorities at a much higher level kept an eye on the situation from afar.

One of Zyne's top executives, Clarence Diamond, listened on a cell phone as his contact within the pentagon relayed instructions. The trial was a success in that it had proven that the infusion could create massive cellular changes capable of creating chaos and death, hence proving to be a powerful weapon in warfare scenarios when the enemy was contained in close quarters. By injecting the infusion into each prisoner, they would kill each other, saving the US military time and money. The element of hair color had been a decoy, but also seemed to be working. It was a bit of a shame, but an understandable trade-off to ensure the creation of an ally for national security.

The inclusion of the celebrities had been anticipated. They'd been hand-selected for a reason. For starters each of them was wanted dead, whether by their own families, or by others in very powerful places. The Zyne Project was the perfect opportunity to get rid of them for the benefit of national security as well as the almighty dollar. And they needed to be famous in order for the conclusion of the trial to make sense. Things were working according to plan. There were only two people Clarence would be reticent to lose...

Dr. Dan Johns and Rosa Rodriguez.

The two had become victims of the study. In order to maintain the highest level of confidentiality, the Pentagon had not revealed the purpose of the study to the CDC and had allowed them to send in one of their own investigators as a precautionary measure.

Damned leak, thought Clarence.

Once the CDC had discovered the trial, the high-profile nature of its subjects, and the danger of rushing to market, they'd intervened, but he'd been told not to worry. It would just be a minor distraction.

As for Dr. Dan Johns, a number of people had tried to convince him to not attend the study. In fact, they had hired a robust team of nurses and technicians to support efforts inside in an attempt to dissuade him from overseeing the trial.

He had—after all—perfected one of the greatest biologic weapons ever constructed...

But now, after listening to instructions, Clarence realized that like the others, Dr. Johns was a drop in the bucket—a minor player in a much larger game.

He also came to the realization that Zyne had just become one of the most powerful corporations in the world.

CHAPTER 7

I t was getting harder to walk...harder to think...
Rosa and Greg made it outside to the pool area, where she motioned for him to sit next to her on one of the plastic white chairs strategically placed in order to catch the best rays of sun. But without the sun, the warm, humid air smelled a bit like plastic and it was difficult to take deep breaths. In the pool, Jennifer had slowly floated to the top and was now facedown in the water, her scalp shiny and red.

The gash on Rosa's forehead started bleeding again and Greg grabbed a towel from one of the chairs, gently pressing it down. The gash was larger now, and as he looked closely, he could see that the skin on her face appeared stretched, with little marks lining her forehead and along the tip of her nose.

Rosa sighed sadly and allowed him to press down on her wound, despite feeling pain from the compression. It actually felt better to close her eyes, because within the past few minutes, she'd been feeling extreme pressure behind each orb. It was a pulsing sensation and she knew, after looking at Rick for nearly an hour that it would only be matter of time, before her poor eyes popped out of the sockets.

Tears formed and dripped down her cheeks. She couldn't believe that she was going to die as a hideous creature. Normal life seemed so far away.

She gently moved Greg's hand away so that she could look him in the eye. "I really appreciate you saving me back there. But I think you should leave me here. I could fully change at any time, and I really don't want to hurt you. It's just that I'm not sure how long it's going to be before I turn into something like Rick."

Greg didn't move. "I'm not leaving you," he replied. "You're sick...yes, I know that. But you're not scaring me, and we've got to try to find a way out. Didn't you say you were able to communicate with the people who have us trapped in here?"

Rosa nodded and pointed to the hole in the tarp. Surprisingly, it had not been covered over by the guardsmen and looked to her like the only beacon of hope in an otherwise yellowish prison.

Greg stood up and walked over to the opening.

"Greg...be careful."

He turned and smiled at her, then directed his attention toward the small hole. He was operating on adrenaline but at times throughout the day had reflected on how this job had turned his life upside down.

Greg was a pretty normal guy. He'd been unlucky enough to work at a Miami manufacturing plant in the product distribution department when the economy tanked, leading to extensive lay-offs throughout the company. When the plant manager had called him in for a 'talk', he'd been aware of his fate, even before any words were spoken.

After losing his job, Greg hunted around for months, searching for anything that would help him pay the bills. Despite living with a roommate in a beaten-down, old apartment, he was finding it financially challenging living on unemployment checks alone.

Then, he'd seen the advertisement online to become a part of the cleaning crew at the Illusions building. For the past year, he'd been helping out in all aspects of facilities—cleaning rooms, sweeping floors, delivering food—there was nothing he wouldn't do.

Life had been getting better. Just getting a regular paycheck helped so much. He'd actually started saving a bit each week and was preparing to get his own place. He was dating a nurse he'd met at the gym and was actually looking forward to life. In fact, right before he'd come to the Illusions building for the new trial, he had enjoyed an intense lovemaking session that had left them both exhausted and happy—they'd been lying in bed and talking about the future.

He remembered how his lover had gently stroked his face as she whispered how much she cared for him in his ear.

Amazing.

But then—this happened—and everything stopped.

Greg was now operating on automatic and knew that he couldn't stop to think too much about the possibilities. He wasn't sure why all of this was happening, but he did know that he couldn't sit around and let the chips fall. He had to take control and part of that meant caring for Rosa while they looked for a way out.

There had to be a way out.

Stepping up on the chair that was positioned underneath the gap in the yellow material, he cupped his mouth and shouted out, "Hello? Can anyone hear me?"

Silence followed, so he tried again, "Hello? Can anyone hear me? We need help!"

Now, there were sounds of gravel crackling and feet shuffling. A loud almost robotic male voice responded through a megaphone, "Sir. We're looking for Dr. Dan Johns. Is he with you?"

Greg thought fast. If he said no, they wouldn't talk with him. However, he wasn't sure exactly how to stall and get more information.

"Yes, he's with us, but he can't talk to you right now. He's treating a patient."

As soon as the words tumbled from his lips, Greg felt ridiculous. *Treating a patient? They'll see right through that*, he thought.

Surprisingly, the voice responded rather quickly. "We understand. But we need to speak with him before we can take any action. When he's done with the patient, please have him come talk with us. Until then, please try to remain calm. Help is on the way."

Rosa moaned in pain and aggravation. She couldn't believe that their captors were repeating the same nonsense they'd said to her.

Greg looked over as if hoping for some guidance, but she was devastated by a reality that was ice-sharp and cutting right down to her soul.

We're all going to die.

Greg wasn't giving up. He tried one more time.

"Please, can you just tell me why you're keeping us locked in here? We're not a danger to anyone."

"Sir," the disembodied voice responded, "It's only a temporary situation. We'll be sending in help shortly. Now, we've got to get back to work, so please only call out to us if you've got Dr. Johns."

Greg wondered if maybe he should impersonate the doctor, but worried that if he was asked a specific question about the infusion that he wasn't able to answer—he might ruin their chances entirely.

Stepping off the chair, he looked back at Rosa and froze. She was sitting up, staring into space, but her mouth was opened in a large O and she was drooling. Suddenly, she fell to the ground and began to shake as if she was having a seizure.

Running over to her, Greg crouched down, unsure what to do. Rosa continued to shake and jerk until she finally gasped and ceased. Lying on the ground, she was positioned in an unnatural angle and stared silently at the sky.

Placing his head down on her chest, Greg checked for a heartbeat. He found one and gently lifted her off the ground, carrying her back inside to the only person who could save her life.

―――――――

Peering into the microscope, Dan prayed for a miracle. The cells were continuing their unusual division, having diluted themselves to watered down replicas. The specimen itself was changing in its texture, becoming watery and strange.

Lying on the table, Rick was continuing to break apart. It was a gruesome sight. His face had now completely broken in half, the skin slowly sliding off the skull, dragging ropey muscle as the flaps methodically slipped down and succumbed to gravity. Piles of useless flesh were now littering the table, creating mountains of grayish-pink lumps.

Turning away from the destroyed man, Dan stumbled and sank down to the ground. He was utterly exhausted and desperate to figure out how to save him. With each passing moment, it was becoming more and more difficult to hang on to hope.

Suddenly, he yawned.

What time is it?

Looking at his watch, he was stunned to see that it was six o'clock in the evening. The day had flown by in a haze of death, panic, and urgency. But now, sitting alone in the laboratory with a creature he had created, the world slowed down and the weight of failure was sitting on his shoulders.

He was beaten.

Suddenly, he remembered that Rosa had spoken with their captors, relaying that they would not speak to anyone but him. Perhaps he could convince them to let everyone out and quarantine the sick...

Dan's thoughts raced as he mentally debated all of the negotiations he could broker to help him escape.

Standing up, he turned to leave when a noise caught his attention. It was a low snarl coming from the direction of the table. Heart pounding suddenly, he slowly pivoted to face the creature.

It was sitting up and staring out into space. With no eyes, it seemed to rely entirely on sound, so Dan tried to be as still as possible. The creature slowly swung its legs over the side, sending piles of rotting flesh to the floor. The skin made a squishy sound as it landed on the linoleum floor in clumps.

The creature moved its mouth...or mouths...as its lips had completely parted now into four discrete sections. Rather than speaking coherent words, it made a painful moaning sound.

Dan was shocked at how swollen and large Rick had become. He was at least double his original size and was still continuing to swell and grow. Dan knew that his organs wouldn't be able to withstand the metamorphosis much longer and would fail. He could hear the creature wheeze as it took in each breath and could tell that complete congestive heart failure was probably going to occur sooner rather than later.

Backing away, Dan reached for his pistol. He didn't want to kill Rick, because if the creature died, he wouldn't be able to observe it to see if the transformation stopped. In addition, he would have to blindly inject Rosa with the solution in hopes that she might be cured.

But there was no choice. The Rick-creature was slowly lowering itself off the table and with a loud *squish* sound, landed on the floor, only a few steps away from him. Dan slowly lifted the pistol and as the melting, swelling nightmare started to approach him, he raised the firearm and shot the creature directly in the head, aiming straight for the brain.

His shot rang out sharply throughout the ruined hallways of the medical center, reverberating off the walls. And there was no drama. Rick fell to the ground and shuddered one last time in a pile of flesh, blood, and ooze.

Shaking, Dan dropped the gun to the floor and stared at the mess in front of him. The creature was actually disintegrating in front of his eyes, shuddering, and melting in a mass of pulsing, dying, flesh. Tearing his gaze away, he staggered out of the laboratory and saw Greg approaching slowly. The man was carrying Rosa in his arms. She appeared to be unconscious.

As the two men neared each other, Dan could see that Greg was sweaty and out of breath. Rosa had also grown due to the metamorphosis and her skin was glistening and stretched under her swelling cells. Her eyes were shut and the gash in her face had deepened and was now stretching out in a vertical direction, similar to the way Rick's face had looked. She was still human and despite her changing appearance, Dan felt sorry for the woman and knew that her time was quickly running out.

"What happened?" he asked Greg.

"She was ok, just in a lot of pain, when she went into a seizure. She fell on the ground and hasn't woken up since. Is there anything you can do for her? Please, you've gotta help her."

Dan looked down and gently touched Rosa's face. Her skin felt like rubber and was hot to the touch. She was in serious distress.

Soon, they would all be in distress as it was growing warmer inside the building and becoming more difficult to breathe.

"Let's put her in Lab C." He quickly shared with Greg that Laboratory A contained the mess that used to be Rick and it would be difficult for them to work in there unless they cleaned it up—a task that no one wanted to perform.

Greg agreed and started to carry Rosa in that direction, but Dan didn't follow right away.

"I'm going to go back outside," he said. "I've gotta give it one more try with those guys to see if I can get some help."

Greg didn't turn around or acknowledge that he heard anything, just continued to trudge toward the laboratory, his precious cargo a virtual deadweight in his arms.

Rosa was dying. It was clear to him by the pallor of her waxy skin and the way her body felt. When Greg placed her on the large mahogany table, her head rolled to one side and she didn't move a muscle. But underneath her skin, he could see little pulsing vibrations.

It was eerie and terrifying.

For the first time all day, Greg had one thought.

I'm not sure I should be alone with her.

CHAPTER 8

It was unbearably hot outside the building in the pool area. Despite the small influx of air passing through the hole cut open by Rosa, the air was humid and fetid—smelling and tasting of a strange type of plastic. The yellowish hue made it even more suffocating, giving off the feel of being stuck inside a large beach ball.

Dan wiped beads of sweat off his brow, feeling thirsty and tired. He didn't have good news to share, but hoped that he could convince Zyne to let them out. He knew that his rights were being violated and wasn't sure if that mattered anymore. Deep down, he knew that there might be something bigger at play.

What if Zyne knew what would happen all along?

The premise shocked him and yet, also seemed possible. The perimeter *had* been secured relatively quickly. Would they have been able to do so with abbreviated notice? Dan pondered that in the midst of all the chaos and activity, he'd not really stopped to think about what was happening. And now, stuck in the midst of the bubble, he could hear all the activity that was occurring outside and started to understand that the activity might have been pre-planned.

Activity that was not waiting for him to administer a cure...

Finding the opening quickly, Dan stepped up on the pool chair and shouted out, "Hello? This is Dr. Dan Johns. Hello?"

He waited a moment, hearing voices in the distance. He could also hear trucks pulling up. It sounded like the vehicles had just arrived at the location. Dan strained to hear what people were saying, but couldn't pick up anything. He could hear the whirring sound of the helicopter overhead. It seemed to be positioned in place and that also worried him. They were locked in like prison inmates, so why were they being guarded so heavily?

Suddenly, a series of gunshots broke the relative calm. Overhead he could hear a robotic voice warning an unseen perpetrator, "Please stay where you are. Do not try to escape."

And then, another loud series of gunfire.

This time, the gunfire sounded mechanical and automatic. The "rat-tat-tat-tat" sound erupted, causing Dan to cover his ears and cower in the chair, terrified that some of the lethal aggression might be pointed in his direction.

Another series of gunfire followed a brief period of silence.

And then...

...all was quiet.

Dan waited in his crouched position for a signal, but this time, all was silent. The trucks weren't moving any longer and the distant chatter he'd picked up had ceased.

Shakily standing up on the chair, he repeated, "Hello? This is Dr. Dan Johns. Is anyone there?"

Then, a voice on a megaphone answered.

"Dr. Johns, please provide an update."

Shouting as loud as he could, he responded to the headless voice.

"We're getting the situation under control. I've identified a biochemical infusion in one of the laboratories that we set aside as a buffer. Right now, we have one subject remaining who will be receiving the infusion shortly..."

He was cut off in mid-sentence.

"Dr. Johns, by 'one subject remaining', are you inferring that the rest of the subjects are dead?"

Dan wasn't sure what to say.

"Dr. Johns, please respond. Are all the other subjects dead?"

"Yes," he replied. "They've all succumbed to cellular abnormalities caused by the infusion."

"Dr. Johns, we appreciate your honesty and for keeping us up-to-date on what's happening in there. At this time, we're going to discuss what next steps should be taken and we'll get back to you. Please come back outside for an update at ten o'clock."

It was seven o'clock. Looking down at his watch, Dan estimated that the sun would be going down shortly and hoped it would help cool things down a bit.

"Given the lack of air, the building is beginning to get very hot. Is there anything you can do?"

"Yes, Dr. Johns. We will cut more holes along the top of the enclosure to give you more oxygen. Please return outside at ten o'clock tonight, and we will give you instructions on how to proceed. We understand you've been stuck inside all day and apologize for the inconvenience, but hopefully we've contained this and can let you out once we've determined how to handle the remaining subject. Do you understand?"

"Yes. Thank you."

Stepping off the chair, Dan felt uneasy. He didn't like the idea of being locked up in the building at night and even though they had electricity, felt somehow safer with daylight still streaming through the yellow-wrapped windows and doors. Now, with the sun beginning to set and the darkness of evening starting to shroud the landscape, he felt as if the darkness would sop up any ray of hope that existed.

As he pushed the doors open and walked back inside, grief spreading through his bones like a malicious cancer. This was not how things were supposed to have turned out. And now, walking through the empty elegant hallways, he felt the gravity of the situation pressing down on his shoulders.

Underneath the darkening sky, large, strange-looking vehicles had pulled up. These were oblong with large cylindrical centers cutting the containers in half. Crews were hooking up wide tubes along the sides of each truck, twisting and torquing each one with careful, precise turns.

Unbeknownst to the people trapped inside, Zyne representatives had left the facility perimeter several hours back. Key executives were transported to private jets with a course set for Washington, D.C. and offices were quickly stripped within a matter of hours by expert cleaners who were dispatched not long after events began unfolding. Laboratory technicians and researchers were asked to leave the premises and not return until requested to do so.

CDC officials were slow to the scene and while Rosa's presence within the clinical trial was not a secret, there were other things to worry about. They'd been briefed that an infusion to treat hair replacement had not gone well and many people had died. In order to ensure safety, all contagious subjects had been quarantined while doctors worked to help them.

The subjects' immediate families were notified that something had gone wrong. Others were notified that everything was proceeding as planned. Some people cried fake tears, others…real. But most of those notified were acutely aware that the death sentences they had helped plan for months were now a reality.

In the meantime, a new slew of people now arrived at the Illusions compound and didn't look anything like scientists or guards.

They were hazardous materials experts — specializing in gases and total sterilization.

The kind of sterilization that did not leave anything left behind.

Total decontamination.

———————

When Dan entered the medical facility, he became immediately aware of how warm everything was. Beads of sweat dripped down his forehead and traveled to his nose, dropping off the tip every so often. It was quiet in the hallway, but as he took a few steps forward, Greg peered around the corner. The man looked tired, but pleased to see him.

Dan was just as relieved to see that he was still alive and that Rosa hadn't woken up completely changed. "How is she doing?" he asked.

"Not great, take a look at her," Greg motioned toward the table.

Rosa looked much worse than before. Her skin had taken on a grayish pallor and her breathing sounded more like wheezing. Her chest rose and fell sporadically as if she was unable to breathe consistently.

Dan knew he would need to get her treated with whatever infusion buffer solution he had left and prayed that she would respond better than Rick had. As he turned to go pick up the vials, Greg grabbed his arm.

"Hey, I need to tell you something else," he said, his eyes serious and wide. "There's something wrong. When I was in here with Rosa, I could hear noises outside. It wasn't clear what I was hearing, but it almost sounded like something sliding against the floor. And then, I also heard some crazy woman laughing. I know it sounds insane, but I really did hear those things."

Dan shook his head, "I heard the gunfire outside, so I'm assuming that our friends with the cleaning crew were trying to escape, but I haven't seen anyone…wait a minute. Didn't you say Jennifer was floating in the pool?"

Greg nodded.

Dan was now very scared.

"Greg. I was just out there. She wasn't in the pool."

The remaining members of the cleaning crew heard it all. In fact, they were now curled up as a group on the floor, hiding behind the bed. They were shaking and everyone was scared.

They had been sitting on the bed, sharing some snacks. One person was on the floor with a blanket, taking a nap. Suddenly, they heard a man moving down the hallway alternately moaning and then hitting the doors as he passed each room.

When he had come past their room, he'd banged on the door.

Thump

Thump

Thump

No one had answered. It was too risky and the man on the other side of the door didn't sound normal. He was huffing and puffing. It also sounded like something was dripping on the carpet.

After several more minutes, the thumping stopped and the man kept walking. One woman sobbed in relief into the sleeve of her shirt.

Her sobs were disturbed by the sound of the man throwing open a door several rooms down. He yelped in victory, and then growled when he realized the room was empty. The group could hear something being thrown against the window followed by the sound of broken glass tinkling and reverberating throughout the hot air.

Then, for the first time all day, they heard a loud voice shouting from somewhere up above, warning everyone to stay put and shooting off mechanical gunfire as reinforcement. Then, they heard more gunfire.

The boldest member of the group, a man named Jimmy, looked out the window and watched as a black flash tumbled to the ground at alarming speed, while gunfire created tiny holes in the yellow tarp, dotting the material as the body fell.

Jimmy couldn't be sure what he was looking at—it all happened so quickly.

But he could have sworn it was Bryan Jackson.

Rosa could hear voices. They sounded distant and muffled, and she recognized both of them. She was in so much pain that coming to her senses was not a pleasant experience. She struggled to remain in the dark where nothing hurt and all she had to do was dream about random, alternate realities. But as each extremity screamed out in pain, she was dragged back into present-day.

Opening one eye, she blinked, trying to focus. Blessed with 20/20 vision her entire life, she was unaccustomed to not being able to see. There was terrible pressure building up behind each eyeball and she felt a strange pounding in her skull as she struggled to focus. As the details of the room came into view, the world seemed hazy and surreal.

An unusual and illogical feeling of rage swept throughout her brain. It came on extremely quickly, filling her with the urge to destroy and gnash and scream. Struggling against the rage, Rosa moaned and twitched on the table, then thrashed, her head whipping back and forth.

Dan ran over and saw her struggle. They didn't have much time.

"Let's restrain her. Quickly."

Greg didn't argue and the two quickly secured her legs by wrapping rope around each ankle. They then strapped her body down to the table and secured each arm with individual pieces of rope. Everything was knotted and secured as tightly as possible.

Rosa tried not to fight them. But the fury was mounting and she could feel her brain fighting against her. It was as if there were two different people at work, both fighting with each other, the angrier of the two winning out.

"Please," she gasped. "Inject me with something to stop...to stop the rage. I'm getting close...and I can't stop it..."

Dan raced to retrieve one of the few remaining sedatives. He quickly filled a syringe and returned just in time. Rosa's eyes were rolling backwards and she had started to drool, spittle emerging out of the right side of her wounded mouth and traveling down her chin.

As the needle plunged forward, the liquid emptied into her veins and Rosa calmed down. But she didn't pass out. Instead, she lay on the table watching them with eyes that had begun to swim and operate independently of each other.

Both men waited for a few moments to see if she would go into convulsions or try to attack them. When neither happened, they both backed away and spoke to each other in hushed voices.

"Dr. Johns, let's give her the infusion. We've gotta try to stop this. Please."

"Yes, of course. But it didn't work on Rick and if it doesn't work on her, I'm just not sure what else I can do."

"I understand," Greg answered, "but it's the only thing left to try. I can't stand watching her turn into one of those things."

Dan sighed and ran his hands through his hair. "Ok. I'll try. Be on your guard. We still don't know where Jennifer is and if there's any chance that these things are reanimating for some reason, you'd better be ready."

Greg held up his knife. "I'm prepared," he said smiling.

Dan chuckled. A knife wasn't going to stop any crazy creature and they both knew it. Still, he did have a gun and if things got bad, he had at least several rounds that he could shoot off before they were completely screwed. He thought about their chances and grimaced.

We're in the hornet's nest. And we're about to get stung.

Outside, the cicadas were singing heartily. The sun had gone down in a diluted, orange haze. The air was thick with heat and the birds flew low, escaping amongst the darkness of the tree limbs.

In the quarantine zone, the work continued.

CHAPTER 9

*D*an still had nightmares about his mother.

Sometimes when he would drink too much and eat a grease-filled meal right before bed, he would dream about his once-beautiful mother. The dreams were always the same...

She'd be greeting guests at a social gathering. The guests would stand around their formal living space, admiring the complex paintings on the wall, the crystal goblets filled with crimson wine, or sometimes, they would swoop down and hold him in their thin, manicured hands—admiring how handsome he was. Such a charming little boy.

His mother would eye the entire event with a cool gaze, her eyes calmly glancing from one end of the room to the other, a hint of a smile painted on her velvet lips. In his dreams, she always looked her best. But he could sense unease within the cool visage. He would look down and see her right ring finger twitching slightly as she casually swayed her hips as if longing to move away.

While in the throes of the dream, Dan would turn his head and revel in the sinister beauty of the moment, reflecting on the cool elegance of the surroundings, and the somewhat distracted, shallow element that surrounded every person like an invisible evil cape.

He would then realize that his mother was gone. She had disappeared, leaving him alone in a false carnival.

Walking quickly out of the room, he would race down the darkened hallway, calling for his mother…

Mommy….Mommy…Mommy…

In the distance, he could hear a silky voice calling to him, "Come here my sweetheart. Come see mommy, Danny. Come see me…"

As he would near the end of the hallway, he'd see her floating toward him; her feet hanging far from the floor—her arms outstretched—the silky fabric of her dress pulled out like wings carrying her forward.

With every passing second, his heart would begin to race with the knowledge that something bad was about to happen.

Something really bad.

Then, as she neared, her face would change and resemble a gargoyle and that gentle, velvet voice would screech as she got closer and closer…

"Come to me Danny….Dannnnyyyyy….."

Dan experienced the same nightmare many times throughout his adult life and wasn't sure why he was remembering it now while rummaging through the laboratory to secure the infusion that might save Rosa's life.

Shaking his head and trying to erase the horrible thoughts of his darkest dreams, he quickly grabbed the last buffer vials. After checking the hallway, he returned to Greg. His unlikely assistant was staring at Rosa with a horrified look on his face and when Dan drew near, he understood why.

Rosa's face had completely split.

The gash that had started along her forehead had now lengthened and split her face in two. Grayish matter oozed out and was pooling around the base of her head. Her eyes were closed, but she was muttering an unintelligible language and alternately moaning quietly.

Dan knew he might be about to lose her and needed to move quickly.

Gently pushing Greg back, he pulled out the syringe and filled it with the last of the infusion buffer. Silently, he approached Rosa and quickly plunged the needle into her arm, emptying the last of the vials...

Thankfully, she didn't budge, just continued to ooze and moan.

Taking a deep breath of relief, Dan staggered back and leaned up against the wall. It was at that moment when he realized how exhausted he was. The nightmare they were living in had positively drained him and the stuffiness of the air inside the building was making it hard to concentrate. All he wanted to do was curl up on one of the couches and take a short nap to clear his mind and regenerate internal batteries that were dangerously low.

He also knew that wasn't an option. Greg was barely hanging on, Rosa was unconscious and turning, and he wasn't completely sure that his other subjects were dead.

They needed to get out—needed to escape.

But he couldn't. He had to try to save Rosa. Like Greg, he felt a kinship to the woman who had hung on so long— certainly longer than the others—and who was fighting against the change to maintain her humanity while her cells worked against her.

He hoped that the infusion would work or at least slow the transformation so that they could get out and provide additional care.

Turning to Greg, he decided it was time to take action.

"I'm going back outside. This is crazy. We can't wait here until ten o'clock for someone to consider letting us out. We need help now."

Greg looked at him with a blank expression. He appeared defeated and exhausted, unable to make a decision.

Dan reached down and gripped his shoulder. "It's going to be ok. Just hang in there. We'll get out of here."

Leaving Greg in the room, he raced down the hallway, and threw open the glass doors to the pool area. Anger flooded his mind. *They can't keep us in here forever*, he thought. *This is absolutely ridiculous. I've got to get us out of here.*

The deck was dark, but automatic lights illuminated the pool. Gentle ripples shimmered along the surface, the table still sitting in the center of the pool partially immersed as a reminder of Rosa's battle with Jennifer. Dan shuddered despite the heat and stepped back up on the chair that was positioned below the hole in the tarp. Inky blackness seeped through the opening and he felt as if he was speaking into a dark abyss to the devil's accomplices.

"Hello?" he shouted. "This is Dr. Johns. I need to speak with someone. Please respond."

This time, he didn't hear any chattering or gravel crunching. The night was silent with the exception of noises that sounded like something rubbing against the ground and people speaking in low voices.

Dan tried again.

"Hello? Is anyone there?"

"HEEELLLLOOO?" he screamed.

Nothing.

No one responded.

Frustrated beyond belief, Dan pulled out the knife he'd been carrying the past several hours as a back-up weapon, and started stabbing away at the hole that Rosa had initially created.

He tore at it with all of his anger and desperation, not caring anymore if someone shot at him. The whole situation had become unbearable and his guilt, coupled with aggravation, was leading him down a crazed, uncaring path.

He'd begun to slash open a considerable hole, when suddenly, the black of night was replaced by a darker black he couldn't quite place. The infinite darkness was still at first and then suddenly pushed out a powerful wave of air that was so strong, it knocked Dan to the ground. Then, the whoosh of air died down and stopped entirely.

Dan found himself lying on the ground and rose unsteadily. The realization of what had just happened hit him like a ton of bricks. Something was now attached to the hole he'd created and had the ability to blow—hard.

It's a trap, he realized. *This whole fucking thing is a trap.*

Sinking back down, Dan realized that there was no getting out. He'd been tricked into trying to save the dying subjects, but his captors on the other side of their prison knew he'd fail. And he knew what that meant.

He'd been a pawn in their game. A game to create the ultimate gene therapy that could kill—turning people into lunatics.

As Dan's brain raced, he realized that the whole operation had been a hoax. Zyne didn't care about changing the world of hair care. They wanted to create something that would be far more profitable.

The guards who are holding us captive are obviously part of the government, he thought. *And they arrived very quickly. They knew we were going to end up like this. What's going to happen to us? And to people like April, who've been so loyal and committed to the project?*

Nausea overtook him then and he turned and vomited into a series of manicured bushes.

Greg was terrified.

Rosa had woken up and was now staring stonily at the ceiling. She was silent and had stopped thrashing. Her stillness frightened him, because she no longer acknowledged that he was in the room. He wasn't sure whether or not her brain had been completely overtaken by the cellular transformation.

Standing up, he walked over to the table, remained a few safe steps away and stared into her face. Her dermis was quickly dissolving and splitting in numerous locations, grayish ooze glistening across nearly every exposed area of skin that hadn't broken apart.

Her eyes frightened him the most.

They were both ruby red and leaking at the corners. Greg wasn't sure if Rosa could still see or if she was just in an angry crimson haze. He hoped the sedatives would keep her under control until Dan returned.

Deep down, Greg had lost all hope. They'd been stuck inside for hours and despite the claim that they might be rescued at ten o'clock, which was a few short hours away, he had a sinking sensation that it was a stall tactic. Why hadn't they been rescued already?

The air was getting hotter by the second and at times, he felt a wave of dizziness wash over him and the world would fall out of focus. He had a feeling that they weren't getting enough oxygen, despite the circulation of the air conditioning throughout the building.

As he stood over Rosa, she slowly turned her head to face him. Her eyes swam back and forth, but it seemed like she might be able to see something, because she was now trying to form a sentence and had started to thrash again.

Suddenly, he heard it.

It sounded like a low moan mixed with an insane laugh. A woman's laugh.

Turning around, his heart stopped.

Jennifer was standing in the doorway. Or at least, what remained of her.

She was wet, water dripping down her head, clothes stuck to her body. But the only reason he could recognize her was because he knew what she had been wearing before the nightmare began. That was the only indication, because she looked very different now.

Jennifer's head was unusually swollen and barely balancing on her neck, swaying from left to right like a metronome. Her eyes bulged out and glared at him. Her skin was completely gray and she resembled a walking corpse—a corpse that was horribly disfigured.

She took a few steps toward him and made the same strange sound again.

Whaa….whaa…

Greg pulled the knife out of his pocket and backed up. He doubted that it would be enough to kill the creature that was slowly approaching, but didn't plan to give up without a fight. As he backed up, he heard something snap and bumped into something wet and squishy.

Rosa had somehow broken free from the rope and was standing right behind him.

Screaming, he tried to get away, but she took him by the arms and threw him against the wall. Connecting with the wall hurt his head, but he quickly realized that she had been trying to protect him.

Rosa was now standing close to Jennifer and snarled at her, ooze dripping down on to the floor and spreading out in a large pool by her feet. The Jennifer-creature lunged forward and the two fell to the floor snarling and gnashing at each other.

110

Rosa managed to grab a hold of Jennifer's swollen head and bashed it into the ground. The two continued struggling, but Rosa took the swollen skull and bashed it into a piece of metal that was holding one of the cabinets in place. It served as a mini-spear and Greg could hear the wet, mushy sound as the metal went right through the skin and bone—into Jennifer's brain. She jerked back and forth for a moment and then stilled.

Rosa rose from the ground, swaying back and forth. She stared at Greg, who remained horrified and backed-up against the wall. She seemed uncertain as to what to do and slowly stumbled out of the room and down the hall.

Dan was entering the medical center when he saw Rosa approach. He pulled the gun and was about to fire when Greg shouted at him, "No, stop!"

Dan was confused. How had Rosa gotten free? And why was Greg protecting her? He kept his gun pointed forward.

"Greg, I'm not sure what's going on here, but we can't just let her leave. She's completely turned and could try to kill us both."

Greg shouted out, "She just saved my life. Jennifer...she came back...and Rosa killed her before she could kill me. Just wait a minute..."

He ran down the hallway after Rosa who had stopped walking. She turned around to face him as he stood just a few inches away.

"Rosa, we want to help you. Please. Don't move...we..."

Suddenly, Rosa reached out and grabbed Greg's head. With one quick motion, she twisted it and pulled it off his neck. Blood spurted out everywhere and the headless body jerked and erupted in spasms, falling to the floor in a loud thud.

Rosa stared at the head she now held and began to stuff it into her mouth, chewing loudly. But her chews were interrupted by a loud shot and her face exploded in one big burst of smoke.

She fell to the ground, still holding Greg's head. When Rosa hit the ground, Greg's head rolled away from her and landed a short distance from Dan's feet.

Dan was still shaking twenty minutes later as he sat alone on the couch in the common area. The scene replayed itself over and over in his head, creating a myriad of horrific images that burned straight through his skull, embedding themselves forever in his aching mind.

As he tried to organize his thoughts, the first thing that hit him was…

I've completely failed.

It was true. All of his subjects were dead. The buffer treatment hadn't worked and his career was over. He'd lost many people and had absolutely nothing to show for it. The "miracle" hair infusion that was supposed to change the face of aesthetics had absolutely fallen flat on its face.

And the worst part about it was that he wasn't sure he was supposed to have succeeded. It had been hours since he'd heard from anyone at Zyne and now the only opening or escape he'd found had been sealed off.

Then, a moment of clarity struck him…

Sitting straight up on the couch, Dan realized that if he could find another exit somewhere within the building to make it outside and cut open another hole large enough to escape through, he might be able to get out. He theorized that in the dark, it would be much more difficult to see small openings appearing in the material.

Dan walked over to the registration area and entered the office. He knew there was a building floor plan posted to the wall for reference and scouring the blueprint, easily found the exit he was looking for.

The loading dock.

On the far west side of the building, the architects had constructed a relatively sophisticated loading dock where trucks could load and unload pallets of food or other necessities. Its shape was awkward in that a large concrete slab jutted out of the entranceway, to provide easy access for different sized trucks and ancillary drayage.

Dan had a feeling that his best chance to escape would be to cut a hole somewhere along the material at ground level because it would be at least partially hidden by the landing that was sticking out. He just needed a knife and a little luck.

Racing back to the kitchen, he found the sharpest knife available and made his way to the back of the building.

When the creature awoke, there was an instant feeling of pain and anger.

It was enclosed in some sort of blanket, which it easily removed and tossed aside. Dried blood flaked off its eyes as they opened and stared into the darkness. Standing up unsteadily, it howled in anger and stumbled into a wall.

A sound caught its attention. It sounded like voices in the distance—but to the creature—it was like nails scraping against a chalkboard.

Furious now, it howled again and stepped out into the hallway, determined to find the source of its anguish.

CHAPTER 10

The remaining members of the cleaning crew were tired, bored, and hungry. They had gone through all of the snacks in the mini-bar, and were feeling restless. Jimmy looked at the two women sitting on the bed together and realized that he should have gone to help Dan and Greg. Sitting like a lame duck waiting for a rescue that might never arrive was simply cowardly.

It's time to take some action.

Standing up, he looked back at the women with a new sense of confidence, perhaps one borne solely out of exhaustion. "I'm going to go out there and see if I can get some help."

Both women stared at him as if he was crazy.

"Are you really going out there?" a woman named Claire asked timidly. "Those things are out there. It's not safe."

Jimmy sighed impatiently. "Well, we're not doing any good staying in here. You see the yellow wrapping covering the windows. For all we know, the government's got us locked in here forever. I don't know about you ladies, but I don't want to die in here. It's starting to get really stuffy and hot too. I think it would be good if we all went out together. That way we can at least watch each other's backs."

"But what about Greg?" asked the other woman, named Leslie.

"I don't know where he is. But what if he's in trouble and we're just sitting here? We've heard all sorts of weird sounds and gunshots. We're putting ourselves in more danger by staying in this room."

The women looked at each other and decided to stay put.

Jimmy sighed and turned around. "Lock the door behind me," he instructed. "And don't open it unless you know it's me."

They both murmured ok and watched as he walked out.

Standing in the hallway, Jimmy realized how good it felt to be out of the room. He'd been going stir-crazy sitting there listening to his female companions weep and worry. Now, being outside by himself, a sweet sense freedom flooded his veins.

His optimism dampened however, when he realized that he was stepping out into the open without anything to defend himself with. Looking around, he thought about checking in one of the rooms, but knew there was nothing around other than bedding and toiletries.

Maybe I could ward off my attacker with a razor, he thought sarcastically.

The elevator was up ahead, but just as he was getting close, he heard a noise in one of the rooms behind him. It sounded strange, likes someone was repeatedly bumping into a wall.

Jimmy weighed his options—he could leave the noise alone and take his chances downstairs, or he could check out the strange sound.

Listening carefully, he couldn't make out any voices—just the strange rhythmic bumping noise.

He decided it was worth checking out and worried that perhaps someone was stuck or in trouble. So he followed the sounds and found himself standing outside one of the rooms. The door was closed and he carefully turned the knob and stepped inside.

The lights were off, making it very hard to see. He could barely see a figure facing the wall. It looked like a man who was slowly banging his hand against the window. After a few moments, the figure backed up, walked toward the window again, banged into it, then stood there for a few more seconds banging on the glass slowly and methodically.

Jimmy watched this happen over and over while his vision cleared and his eyes grew accustomed to the dark. The scene was bizarre and mesmerizing, yet a small voice in the back of his head was quietly screaming 'Get out! Get out!'

Suddenly the bizarre repetitive dance stopped and the man stood staring at the wall. Jimmy finally shook himself out of his reverie and began to back up. The silhouetted man turned around and it was then that Jimmy realized something was very wrong.

He started to scream, but it didn't last very long.

CHAPTER 11

First came the screams…

Claire and Leslie covered their ears and sobbed as the sounds of death and violence erupted several rooms away from them. They held each other tightly and waited for the inevitable.

Then…came the knock.

It was slow and seemed to linger as if the person on the other side of the door was sliding a hand up and down the frame.

Knock

Knock

Knock

"Maybe it's Jimmy and he's hurt," whispered Claire. "We can't leave him out there."

Leslie glared angrily and whispered back, "Are you fucking crazy? We can't open the door. We don't know what the hell's out there. What if it's one of those crazy people trying to get in? You know what Jimmy said…he said he saw that black guy,

Bryan Jackson, jump out of the window. And there's all those other people running around out there."

Claire went over to the door and asked carefully, "Who's there?"

Nobody replied, but as she turned back around someone knocked on the door again—and this time it was harder and with more purpose.

"Oh shit," she whispered. "What the hell do we do?"

Leslie was about to reply, when the door burst open. Splinters of wood flew out in every direction and the door hit the wall with ferocity.

Both women shrieked and crawled under the bed, curling up against each other and frightened beyond words. From their vantage point, they could hear someone moaning and grumbling and saw two sneakers appear in the doorway. The sneakers were stained red and very dirty.

As the sneakers moved forward, they watched as the intruder entered their room. They could tell that it was a man and that he was injured because he was walking strangely. Instead of lifting up his feet to take steps forward, he was dragging his right foot along the ground. Claire thought it was possible that the man had broken his foot while kicking the door down.

They watched and held their breath as he shuffled past the bed and went to the window. The man began pounding on the glass with the palm of his hand. The sound reverberated throughout the room and both women tried to remain as still as possible to avoid detection. They weren't sure what they were facing, so it was easier to remain silent and pray.

The thumping finally stopped and it sounded like the man was going into the bathroom. Claire and Leslie looked toward the open door and a silent agreement passed between them. It was time to escape.

Suddenly, Leslie screamed. Claire watched in horror as the man dragged her out from under the bed. As the woman's face disappeared from view, Claire didn't hesitate. She crawled to the other side of the bed and ran out of the room, Leslie's screams echoing in the air behind her.

Dan moved slowly across the building. From the blueprints, he knew that to get to the loading dock, he would need to pass through several backdoor areas and service entrances. And frankly, he wasn't sure what he was going to find.

But his fears were unfounded. He discovered that most of the service people, with the exception of the medical clinic personnel, had left. It was unusual because at any one time, he'd been told that a general group would remain on location to ensure that the subjects always had access to clean bedding, food, and amenities.

He thought back to when he'd made his first phone call to Zyne. At the time, it had seemed like there were more people around. Had a group of people left before the doors were locked and closed off? Dan knew that the building automatically locked up in the event of a disaster and that Zyne security was the only group that could control access.

So, it was possible that a group had been alerted to leave…

Dan quickened his pace. He was beginning to feel like a rat in a maze.

Turning a blind corner, he ran smack into Claire who had decided to escape down the back stairwell instead of taking the elevator. Her hair was plastered down by sweat and she was red-faced.

"Dr. Johns," she gasped. "Upstairs…"

She couldn't continue, so he held her in his arms as she sobbed uncontrollably. When she was finally spent and able to speak, she stared at him with swollen eyes and told him about the assailant upstairs.

Dan thought quickly. Who was still unaccounted for?

Rick, Rosa, Jennifer, Teresa...they were all dead.

That only left Bryan...and...Tim.

Dan hadn't seen either of them. He knew that Tim was dead and wrapped up in one of the sleeping rooms upstairs, but given what he'd seen and the fact that Jennifer reanimated, anything was possible. So, he tried to get a description from Claire.

"Well," she said, "I was really trying to get out of there. All I could see was this bald guy with...well, his head looked really strange. Kinda swollen and egg-shaped."

"Was he black or white?"

"Oh, he was white. I could at least see that. But he was also kind of red and swollen. He looked awful...really sick."

Or dead, thought Dan. But he knew better than to divulge that piece of information given Claire's mental state. He needed her calm and rational so that they could both escape. And there was no doubt that she was describing the only remaining subject unaccounted for.

Tim.

The surfer had somehow reanimated after being stabbed to death. Dan wasn't sure exactly what element of the gene therapy was allowing this to happen, but was only too aware that once cell manipulation began—anything could happen.

Swallowing hard, he tried to remember how long it had taken Rick to essentially disintegrate. He had turned shortly before Tim, so perhaps the surfer would find himself in the same situation and not pose as much of a threat.

Dan knew, however, that there were many unknowns and the effects of the gene therapy could create unimaginable situations. He resigned himself to the fact that the only thing to do now was to plow forward, and bring Claire with him. Kneeling down in front of her, he spoke softly and directly.

"Claire, please listen to me. We can't stay here. We've got to try to get out. Do you understand?"

Claire nodded numbly.

Dan continued. "We're going to go over to the loading dock, which is down the hallway. Once we get outside, it's going to be dark and hot, but I need you to stay quiet and let me do what I've gotta do. I'm going to try to cut a hole in the tarp so that we can escape. But you've got to be quiet. Ok?"

The woman appeared to be in shock, so Dan gently rubbed her shoulder and stood up. Then, he carefully led her down the darkened, empty hallways until they reached their destination.

A closed door entitled "Dock" indicated that they were in the right place. As Dan reached for the door, the two could hear what sounded like a man howling in the distance. Claire looked terrified, so Dan took her hand and pulled her through the doorway.

As they stepped outside, they were encased by a dull yellow glow. The lighting along the dock was set on an automatic timer and immediately turned on at seven o'clock. Dirty bulbs lined the walls in different spots, casting weak rays of light that reflected off the covering that surrounded the building. The overhanging tarp created a small space to move around on the landing, but at the ground level, the floor was a dark pit of nothingness.

Pulling out his knife, Dan walked to the edge of the landing and found a piece of material that was hanging down. Due to the contrast from the artificial lighting, it was impossible to tell if the perimeter was lit from the outside, so the doctor took a deep breath and quickly grasped the material, poking the knife into it over and over, until he finally popped a hole through the covering.

Prepared for gunfire, he jumped back quickly and waited.

The night was silent, with only the distant ambient sounds of activity rumbling in the distance. A surge of hope rose in his chest.

This might actually work.

Dan walked over to the edge of the landing and found a small series of steps that led to the ground. Motioning for Claire to remain where she was and keep quiet, he crept down the stairs and found himself standing on soft grass, interrupted in different places by tiny gravel. Lowering himself to the ground, he crawled along until he reached a spot of material that had been fixed to the ground by a spike.

Dan pushed the knife against the material and once again, made a small hole in the tarp. He began painstakingly tearing the hole open slowly and deliberately.

———

Standing up on the landing, Claire tried to focus and calm her racing nerves. She was terrified that the man she'd seen upstairs would find them and was only too aware that the howling in the distance was his angry call.

She had escaped, and he knew it.

Standing outside alone wasn't calming her nerves either. She'd nearly had a heart attack when Dan cut out his "test" hole and unhappily waited as he went down the stairs in search of a hidden area they could use as an escape route. Claire could hear Dan in the distance as he dropped to the grass and began to work on the material once again with his knife.

Looking up, all she could see was yellowish material hanging overhead. Dan was right. It was hot and stuffy. Claire had never been prone to claustrophobia but she could feel the tight quarters begin to press in on her as small beads of sweat formed and quickly dripped down the sides of her face.

Feeling faint all of a sudden from the heat and stress, she decided to lean against the door. Pushing her back against the wooden frame, she sighed and closed her eyes. The sound of Dan sawing away against the material and the distant outdoor noises were strangely soothing and amazingly, Claire found herself dozing off.

A low hum in the distance slowly caught her attention. At first it was very peaceful and seemed far away. It was soothing and pleasant. Almost like a foghorn singing a mournful melody in the hazy shroud of an early dawn stretching across a quiet lake.

But the humming grew louder and warning bells began ringing in Claire's mind. Straining to hear, she opened her eyes and pressed her ear against the door. The humming was actually moaning and every so often she could hear a frustrated, angry bellowing in the distance.

"Dr. Johns," she whispered loudly. When he didn't answer she went to the edge of the landing and could see him quickly sawing away at a small but growing hole. "Dr. Johns!" she whispered again, this time more urgently.

Dan looked up from his work to see Claire silhouetted against the darkened, eerie lighting.

"What?" he asked irritated, not wanting to stop working on what might be their only chance for an escape route.

"I heard something on the other side of the door. I don't think we're safe. It sounds like that man again."

Suddenly a loud crash made them both jump. Turning around, Claire could see that the door was still closed, but she wasn't sure for how long. Racing down the steps, she motioned in the other direction.

"We've got to hide. That thing is close by," she whispered, tears welling up in the corners of her eyes.

Dan considered his options. If they made too much noise, the guards would figure out what was going on. But if Tim came crashing outside, it wouldn't matter. Their cover would be blown.

They really had no choice.

"Ok," he agreed. "Let's leave the building, but be very careful. Any weird movement, and we'll be discovered."

Claire nodded and followed the doctor as they pressed their bodies tightly against the wall and slowly made their way south—away from sounds that reminded them of how fragile their lives were.

The creature that had been Tim was furious and confused.

The world was a red haze of anger and hunger. It was mad and wanted to kill and destroy, yet was in a never-ending swell of pain. As it lumbered down the hallway, it could smell the people who had once been there. A combination of acrid sweat, fading perfume, and body odors tortured its nostrils.

As it moved, a trail of slime followed behind it. The thing no longer resembled the surfer's easy manner. The cellular activity deep within its swelling body was creating intense regeneration that was too much for the outer layers of skin to keep up with. Every orifice was growing, while the dermis was breaking apart from the tension. The cells were filling with water and dividing...again and again...

But the creature, despite its reanimation and handicaps, could hear very well. And the sound of shoes scraping against gravel sounded amplified to its wounded ears.

It needed the sounds to stop.

Furious, it growled and then screeched at the top of its lungs. Up ahead, it could see a door in the distance. The creature raced toward it.

CHAPTER 12

It was nine o'clock.

The perimeter surrounding the Illusions building had been pushed back more than a mile. The media was furious. They'd been standing around all day, conducting live shots with a clear view of the building behind them, glowing yellow in the hot Florida heat.

But now, their live shots would be happening in the dark without any background visuals at all. The group had been moved out to the highway and wasn't being told why. National guardsmen closed off the road, putting up cones to block any incoming traffic.

Once the civilians left the perimeter, the final phase began.

CHAPTER 13

As Dan and Claire carefully crept along the outside of the building, they began to hear strange sounds. And then they watched as the tarp began to shake and shift. It seemed as if it was being manipulated at one end and then another.

Whatever was going on, they were in the wrong place.

"We need to get back inside," whispered Dan. "If they're letting us out, we need to get back to the pool area."

Unfortunately, they were on the wrong side of the building. The pool deck, along with all of the other guest amenities were strategically located on the other side of the building, away from all of the service entrances, loading docks, and off-loading ramps.

"How are we going to get back in?" Claire asked. She hadn't seen any doorways along the wall since they'd left the loading dock.

Dan sighed and looked down.

"We're going to have to go back where we came from."

"What?"

"I know, I know. We don't know if it's safe. But we don't have a choice. If we keep on going in this direction, we'll end up at the entrance and then have to walk all the way around to the other side. It'll be much faster if we cut across."

Claire was silent. She wasn't sure she agreed with him.

"Look, I'm going back. If you want to stay here, hidden in the dark, I'll come back for you."

Looking around, Claire decided that she felt safer hiding in the dark, than returning toward what she felt was imminent danger. She didn't want to be alone, but figured if she waited, Dan would come back for her.

"Ok, but you promise to come back for me, right?" she asked hesitantly.

"Yes. But take this for protection." Dan handed her the gun. "And don't hesitate to use it if you need to."

Claire took the gun slowly and stared at him with wide, sad eyes. He suddenly felt horrible, realizing how many lives had been impacted by his mistake.

Leaning back against the wall, he said softly, "Look, I'm so sorry. I've fucked up royally and now you have to pay for it. Hopefully, we can both make it out of here alive and I promise you, I'll make it right."

Claire didn't know what to say. She wasn't sure why the doctor was apologizing to her—a lowly member of the cleaning staff. But he was handsome and sincere, so she felt inclined to give him the solace he was so desperately seeking.

"It's ok," she said and reached out, gently stroking his cheek.

Dan blinked, surprised at her gesture, but appreciated it. He came closer and hugged her tight. The human contact felt good and comforting. As he held her, he could smell the faintest of perfume along her neck and dug his face into her hair, breathing in her femininity.

You're acting crazy and desperate, a soft voice whispered in the back of his mind, but Dan ignored it. He knew that every moment left was fleeting and was determined to pull comfort from this kind, pretty woman who didn't openly blame him for this disaster...

Pulling back from Claire, Dan looked into her face and realized that she was very attractive. His groin tingled and he felt a stirring that didn't belong in such a dark, ominous place. But still, he was attracted to her. Leaning forward, he kissed her lips gently.

She didn't resist and allowed him to pull her against him once more, as they kissed more fervently, his tongue parting her lips.

He gently pushed her up against the wall and kissed her again and again, pushing his hips into hers. They squirmed against each other, seeking pleasure and...escape...

But their kissing was disturbed by the tarp once again shifting and moving. Dan stopped breathlessly and looked at Claire, who seemed so small and fragile...

"Are you sure you want to stay here? Come with me."

But despite her arousal, a sharp blade of fear was still lodged squarely in her heart. Claire knew that if she followed the doctor, it might take her closer to the creature that had killed her co-worker and friend.

It just wasn't worth it.

"No. I'm ok. I'm going to stay here. Don't worry, I'll be fine. Just come get me when you reach help. I'll stay right here."

He really didn't want to leave her, but knew that if they were going to survive this, he needed to move quickly.

Kissing her again on the lips, he gave Claire one last hug and promised to return as quickly as possible.

Moving slowly toward the dock and feeling euphoric from kissing Claire, Dan felt hopeful once more, despite the obvious danger of possibly bumping into Tim. He could see the yellow glow from the loading dock emanating from up above and stopped, breathing heavily, and waited to see if anything jumped out or growled at him.

Nothing happened. But he could still hear the tarp rustling in the distance. Moving quickly up the stairs, he reached the landing and stopped.

The door was open.

Dan looked around wildly.

Perhaps the creature came outside and then went back in? he wondered.

He neared the entranceway and peered inside. The hallway was empty, so he stepped in and carefully made his way to the other side of the building. Amazingly, the building was still lit, but the air was very stuffy and once in a while, he could hear scraping noises outside.

What the hell is going on?

It took an agonizing seven minutes to get from one end of the building to the other, but Dan finally made it to the pool deck. When he pushed open the glass doors, the first thing he noticed was the hole he had cut open was now considerably larger. He could also see that the entire area was brightly lit by artificial lights and dark objects cast large shadows across the material.

There were men yelling and speaking quickly.

Suddenly, a megaphone in the distance called out, "Project Zyne active. Countdown commencing...five, four, three, two...one."

Dan listened as a siren rang out and then it sounded like hundreds of generators turned on. The ground rumbled beneath his feet and it was only when tendrils of smoke started to appear in the opening that he realized his mistake.

———————

Claire stood in the darkness and wondered if she had made the right decision. Kissing Dan had been a surprise—a nice one. She smiled and wondered if perhaps when all was said and done, she might have a chance with him.

Mom will be so excited. He's a scientist and a doctor. Can you imagine? She smiled to herself.

Claire was a simple, but hopeful woman. She had moved to South Florida from Des Moines in search of more excitement and a change in life. But without a college degree, her options had been limited. Working at Illusions was a way to pay the bills until she could secure a more firm position.

Dating had been tough too.

She thought about going out on a date with a man who could actually pay for the meal. The guys she typically went out with weren't exactly loaded. But Dr. Dan Johns was different. He was someone who was educated, handsome, and local.

And he was a good kisser…

Claire's pleasant delusion was abruptly cut short by the sound of a low growl. Chills ran up her spine and her bladder loosened as she looked around.

Gripping the gun, she peered anxiously into the darkness. It was hard to make out anything in the distance, but she could hear someone else breathing and watching her.

Suddenly she heard the growl again and this time, the Tim-creature emerged. It was bloated and clumsy as it stumbled toward her, arms outstretched and fingers twitching, desperate to tear her apart.

Claire screamed and backed up. Forgetting about the gun, she panicked and ran in the opposite direction.

Her body scraped against the tarp as she ran past the building, her feet slipping on stones. She stumbled a few times and accidentally dropped the gun, but despite the burning in her lungs, she didn't stop. She kept on running until she reached the front of the building.

To her horror, there was smoke slowly pouring into the air from a hole in the material, making it impossible to breathe.

Coughing, she tore off her shirt and pressed it against her mouth as she'd been instructed to do during Zyne fire hazard training and ran toward the pool area.

Dan watched from inside the building as smoke began filling the pool deck. His heart raced as the realization of their predicament poured into his mind.

There was no rescue. Zyne didn't want any survivors.

The company wanted them dead.

Well, thought Dan. *I'll be damned if I'm going to let them kill me. We're going to survive…*

He turned to go when suddenly he heard banging and scraping noises outside. Turning to the glass, he saw Claire stumbling around the pool deck. She couldn't breathe and was alternatively coughing and banging into the furniture. To make matters worse, she was topless and was stumbling around in just a bra, clutching a shirt to her nose and mouth.

Dan threw the doors open just in time to catch her fall as she tumbled into his arms in a dead faint.

He carried her inside and managed to shut the doors behind him, blocking out the smoke for the time being. Rushing into the common room, he put her gently down on the couch and ran to the sink to get some cold water. Once he had saturated a cloth, he came back and wiped down her forehead and cheeks as she slowly came to her senses.

"Where...?" was all she could make out before falling into a coughing fit.

He held her gently and stroked her hair until the coughing ceased and she was able to focus.

"You're ok now. You're ok," he repeated.

"He's out there," she whispered, pointing to the doors.

Dan stood up for a moment and went back to the pool entrance. Locking the glass doors manually from the inside, he peered out into what was becoming a smoky haze. In the distance, he could see someone hobbling around.

Horrified, he realized it was Tim. But the creature wasn't doing well. It was coughing heavily and turning blue from lack of oxygen. As it neared the glass, Dan backed away, but got a clear look at its face, or what had once been a face.

The creature's face had split in so many places that it looked as if it had been pushed up against a gas grill and allowed to sizzle for several minutes. One of its eyes was missing, the remaining orb a red, watery mess. It was shooting out ooze every time it took a breath, and it appeared to be suffocating. The cut in its neck that Dan had given it hours ago and that should have been deadly appeared to have coagulated. Gasping, the creature banged against the doors, its hands slipping against the smooth surface as it fell lower and lower to the ground. Finally on its knees, it banged on the glass one more time, opening its mouth in a pained, unsuccessful attempt to draw in oxygen.

It finally fell to the ground and stilled. And this time, it did not get up again.

It's lack of oxygen, thought Dan sardonically. *Without oxygen, the cells cannot divide and reanimate. That's the only way to cure them. Suffocate them or destroy their brains.*

Backing away from the glass, Dan knew it was only a matter of time before the smoke entered the building and polluted all of the available air. He could already faintly smell a burning scent causing his heart rate to increase.

We've got to get out of here, he thought.

Claire watched Dan as he ran out of the room. She felt extremely weak and fatigued. The smoke had literally come out of nowhere and had enveloped all of the available oxygen. At first, she'd been able to breathe it in and not cough, but after a few moments, had found her lungs closing up—forcing her to find available air. Covering her mouth with her T-shirt had only helped for a few minutes—a strange chemical flavor quickly found its way through her shirt shortly after.

She was lucky to be alive and said a little thank you to the heavens that Dan had found her so quickly. Closing her eyes, she tried to relax for a moment and became acutely aware of the fact that her mind was hazy and her muscles felt twitchy and strange.

Trying to ignore the effects of the smoke, she opened her eyes when she heard Dan reappear. He looked tired and worried. And she knew why. They wouldn't last long with smoke pouring into the building. She felt like crying, but couldn't force any tears out.

As her father used to say, *Looks like we're toast babycakes.*

"Ok, here's what we're going to do," Dan said breathlessly as he neared the couch. "We've got to get out of the building and back to where I was cutting that hole. Hopefully we can get enough oxygen to keep us conscious until we're able to get out. Are you able to walk?"

Claire nodded and he helped her off the couch. As she stood up, he pulled her close to him and they kissed gently and full of emotion. She felt vulnerable standing in front of him in only a bra, but Dan did not appear to notice and focused his attention on her eyes.

"You're going to be ok. And this time, I'm not going to leave you. You're sticking with me. Got that?"

Claire simply nodded again and took his hand as they raced out of the room, back to the loading dock.

When they reached the door to the loading dock, they were already feeling sick from the smoke. The air in the building had grown hazy and warm, making it impossible to tolerate for more than a few minutes. Claire was once again pressing her shirt against her nose and mouth, trying to filter the air as best as possible.

She was feeling strange. At times, it felt as if her muscles wouldn't listen to her and she tripped while quickly walking. At other times, she felt drunk and woozy. Not saying anything to Dan, she continued to follow him out of the building but wondered if there was something wrong with her.

As they stepped out on to the landing, they both stopped for a quick breath. The air in this area wasn't as smoky, but it was definitely not clean and continued to exude the same burning smell. Motioning to remain as quiet as possible, Dan held out his hand and led Claire down the stairs. Much to their relief, the hole that Dan had cut open hadn't been discovered and the air that flowed through it was humid and clean.

They both took turns breathing through the hole and Dan continued cutting it. He worked hard and quickly, completely aware that every moment he delayed could cost them their lives.

Claire watched him and tried to keep from coughing. As each minute passed, the air got tougher to tolerate. But any strange or abrupt sound could draw attention to their location, so she kept her breathing shallow and coughed into the T-shirt when she could no longer bear it.

After about fifteen minutes, she heard Dan whisper, "Claire, I think we can fit through."

Looking at his handiwork, she was impressed. The hole was indeed large enough for them to wriggle through. Feeling a bit of relief, she moved toward him and prepared to try to push herself through the hole, when suddenly they heard a growl.

They looked at each other. Who could possibly still be alive?

In the darkness, a shape on the ground wriggled. It was hard to see at first, but then as it moved into view, Dan saw the Zyne Project's last remaining subject...

Bryan.

But it was no longer the Bryan he remembered.

The fall from the window had broken all of its legs and arms so it was basically wriggling on the ground like an overgrown centipede, trying to make it to oxygen. Dan already knew that the creature would attack them and draw attention to their hiding place, so he did the only thing he could think of to make sure they'd be safe.

Grabbing the knife out of his pocket, he carefully walked up to the creature, lifted the weapon up in the air and brought it crashing down on the disintegrating skull, bursting bone and finding the atrophying brain. Dan could feel the bones crunch and the oozing softness of the brain as the knife plowed through the creature's head. Ooze splattered everywhere, and shot up into Dan's eyes.

He turned away and vomited all over the floor, stumbling backwards and away from Bryan.

When he turned to look at Claire, he was shocked to find her lying on the ground, twitching. He raced over and found that her head was positioned on its side. She was frothing at the mouth and her eyes had rolled back into the sockets.

Stepping back with a sob, he realized that the smoke filling the air was actually mixed with gas.

Nerve gas.

He couldn't watch Claire die. It was too much for him and every moment that he hesitated, would bring him closer to death. Now, pulling and cutting the tarp with every ounce of strength left in his body, he was able to poke his head through.

Uncaring as to whether he lived or died, he waited for gunfire to blow his brains out.

But nothing happened.

Dan decided he couldn't wait another moment and shoved his entire body through the hole, dropping to the ground. He was in a darkened area of the building, shrouded by trees and the dumpster. But the guards weren't far away and he knew it would be only moments before his escape was detected.

Running as quickly as he could, he raced toward the trees and hid in the woods. He watched as the army helicopter that was circling overhead, suddenly stopped moving and held its position. Seconds later, he could see a ray of bright light positioned near his escape route and heard voices shouting in the distance.

Not waiting another minute, he ran deeper into the woods, searching for a better place to hide. As the branches and trees scratched at his exposed skin, he squinted in the dark to see if there was anywhere he could rest.

A gaping darkness underneath a large tree with exposed roots provided him with the shelter he needed. Dropping to the ground, Dan managed to crawl underneath the tree and position himself in the tiny cave. He curled up in a ball, covering his head with both arms.

Dan wasn't sure if he was praying for life...or death.

CHAPTER 14

"What do you mean someone escaped?"

"Well, sir…we've located a hole along the west side of the building. It's large enough for someone to pass through…"

"And why wasn't this detected sooner?"

"Well, sir…we're not sure. We've been scouring the area for hours. It appears that the hole is in an area close to the ground that remained…well…undetected."

"This is unacceptable. We must find any survivors. Do you understand me?"

"Yes, sir. Right away, sir."

Clarence was seated at the head of the table in the conference room, when his cell phone rang. Motioning for the discussion to cease, he answered the phone, recognizing the Army Sergeant's number immediately.

"Yes?"

Listening carefully, his brow furrowed as the Sergeant relayed the situation. He barely spoke, with only a few "Yes's" and "No's" escaping from his lips. Once the conversation was over, he hung up the phone and faced the other members of the executive committee.

"Gentlemen, it appears we have a situation. During the quarantine, some of the subjects may have escaped."

The others in the room began to twitch in their chairs and appeared extremely nervous.

"So, what should we do?" one of them asked.

"Do we need to give a statement?" another questioned.

Clarence sat back and gave the group a small smile.

"Gentlemen, please calm down. As I said, we had a few subjects escape, but the fact remains that the perimeter is secure and they won't get far. We did ensure that even escaping wouldn't put us at risk. Remember?"

Slowly, the members of the executive committee began to relax and as the realization set in, they each began to smile and sit back comfortably in their chairs.

CHAPTER 15

When Dan awoke, he wasn't sure where he was at first. It was dark, cramped, and every muscle ached. He was also incredibly thirsty and his mouth felt parched. His throat was sore and it hurt to swallow. To top it off, he needed a piss.

Stepping out of the hole, he looked around. At first, he'd heard voices and lights in the distance as guards searched for him. But several hours later, the search had been called off and everyone returned back to the building to finish the quarantine activities.

Or in this case, the termination process…

Dan wasn't sure why everyone had disappeared, but once he tried to stand up and relieve himself, clarity washed away any questions that had clouded his mind.

He could barely stand up.

His muscles were twitching badly and once fully upright, he felt extremely sick and weak. And he knew why.

The nerve gas.

They had asked him to take a look at nerve gas when he was working at the laboratory, shortly after the Zyne Project had started. It was a special type of gas that not only caused severe neurodamage but also robbed the body of all of its oxygen within a matter of hours. Some people called it the "Silent Suffocater."

He remembered how one of the top guys, some suit-and-tie-type named Clarence, had come in and asked to chat for a moment.

"How's the infusion going?" Clarence had asked.

Dan had responded positively. He knew that there was still a ways to go, but these guys paid very well and he needed them to support his efforts. Plus, he was working with baseline formulas they'd created and was just making things work better—putting the whole show together in a concise, safe formula.

Clarence had listened to his scientific babble for a while and then swiftly changed the subject.

"Dr. Johns, we're thinking about taking this to the clinical trials stage, but we know that as with any gene therapy, there are dangers. We've been investigating different types of gases that we could give our test subjects if they experience pain or muscle discomfort as a result of the therapy. As you know, we want to ensure that they are as comfortable as possible, given their celebrity status."

Dan had nodded and believed the entire story.

"But we know that there are dangers associated with different types of gases," Clarence had continued, "and we need to be absolutely sure we can discern and steer clear of the ones with deadly elements. We don't know exactly how this therapy is going to interact with chemicals, so it would be a great help to us, if you'd do some testing to see which gases work best in terms of pain management and which ones we need to avoid."

Hours spent testing chemicals against the infusion led to the understanding that some gases were fine, but others, like the ones used by the army or other militia, could have debilitating effects. And nerve gases, particularly 'The Silent Suffocater' would be irreversible and ultimately fatal if ingested in large quantities for an extended time period.

Dan leaned up against the tree, feeling weakness in his arms and legs.

No wonder they've stopped looking for me, he thought. *I'm already dead.*

CHAPTER 16

C rews filled the entire building with gas. They continued their efforts until smoke emanated from every spot and they could see that the tarp was extending out from the air pressure inside. At that time, the vents were shut off and then began to operate in reverse; sucking all of the air out of the building. A few windows shattered from the force of the extraction, but otherwise, everything remained.

When that was complete, a new set of workers arrived and within an hour, had removed the tarp.

Once the building was bare, they created a fire line around the perimeter. They burned everything—the bodies on the lawn, the building—everything inside was destroyed.

In essence, all available evidence was extinguished.

The flames licked and tore at Claire's body. But she was already dead.

Tim and Bryan were destroyed and once the fire reached the building, it found every dead subject and ate away at lives that just days ago, had been vibrant and hopeful.

Families of the victims watched the government bonfire on TV. Despite the media being pushed back, the fire was clearly visible. Flames reached toward the sky behind reporters who remained in the darkness clutching their microphones. Some family members wept and vowed to sue, but the majority of them knew better. They had commitments from the government and from Zyne and would be paid handsomely for their secret participation.

Representatives from the Zyne Corporation returned to the scene and gave their statements, claiming that the doctor who had organized the entire operation, Dr. Dan Johns, had gone rogue and held the subjects hostage. He'd demanded to be remunerated—wanted $50 million dollars in order to release his famous subjects—but when his demands had not been satisfied quickly enough, he'd torched the building and killed everyone inside—

—everyone, including himself.

The local reporters quickly regurgitated the story to their captive audiences and flashed photos on the screen of those lost in the fire:

Rosa, with her beautiful raven hair and gentle smile. A member of the CDC, on hand to make sure everything went safely.

Rick, the owner of a large thriving hair replacement business. Described as ambitious, friendly, and always willing to negotiate a good deal to help his customers get their hair back.

Jennifer, the socialite whose face had graced countless tabloid magazines. A jaded blonde, looking for a new start in life.

Teresa, the online travel industry's businesswoman of the year.

Bryan, the star athlete with a glowing future in front of him.

Tim, the cool surfer who could hang with the best of them and wrangle even the highest and deadliest of waves.

And...

Dan, the mad scientist and doctor who lost his mind in pursuit of the answer to hair color manipulation and who killed many hapless victims after his financial demands were unmet.

All wanted dead. All human guinea pigs in a secret government test that went *exactly* as planned.

Reporters barely mentioned Claire, Greg, the other members of the cleaning crew, or the handful of technicians and nurses who'd lost their lives. There was also no mention of the strange disappearance of some Zyne laboratory employees, who had mysteriously resigned during the incident and moved away.

Their bodies, now floating at the bottom of the Atlantic Ocean, would never be found.

All of the commotion and media hoopla was lost on Dan. He was trying, albeit unsuccessfully, to make it out of the perimeter. Every step he took felt like bricks of lead were shoved in his shoes and it was getting more and more difficult to breathe.

Watching the building explode in the distance broke his heart. He knew that Claire was lying in the grass, her beautiful body melting as the fire tore into her skin. With sadness, he realized that he'd never even gotten her last name.

Time was running out. From the studies he'd done, he knew that he only had about one hour left at the most, before his entire body would shut down. The chemicals were already racing through his bloodstream and wreaking havoc on his nerves while starving his cells of oxygen.

Eventually, the overload would be too much and everything would just...stop.

It was easier to crawl, so Dan got on his hands and knees and slowly made progress. He crawled for nearly twenty minutes when he saw dim light shining through the trees.

I've reached the road, he thought, almost crying out with relief.

Inching forward, he finally made it to the street and fell face forward on the asphalt. To his surprise, this part of the road was not closed off. He figured that once the media had reported on the scene, the government had opened the lanes of traffic.

Unable to move anymore, he turned his head and saw a bright light coming toward him. With every last ounce of strength in his body, he lifted up his arm and tried to flag down the car. When he saw the vehicle slow down on approach, he closed his eyes and allowed darkness to overtake him.

SIX MONTHS LATER

C larence was extremely satisfied with his life.

After the Zyne Project was complete, there'd been quite a bit of activity. He signed the contract—giving the government full proprietary rights to the "Z" formula as well as the ability to continue testing the formula in his facility if necessary.

In addition, the Zyne Corporation decided to focus on its existing product lines and redirect money out of Research and Development for a while. They shared with the staff that given the recent tragedy at the Illusions building, they were going to focus the company on its aesthetic, traditional product lines and consider investing in R&D at a later time.

Magically, despite the recent tragedies, both Zyne and the military came out virtually unscathed.

Settlements between Zyne and the grieving families were reached, but public opinion regarding the corporation did not veer negatively, given the numerous fundraising and community relations efforts the company undertook following the incident.

The fact that Dr. Dan Johns had gone absolutely "off his rocker" as many described it, despite having a stellar record and being highly recommended, shielded Zyne from further negativity. Many felt that the man was a "bomb waiting to go off" and that Zyne executives wouldn't have been able to predict the man's unusual behavior, given that he'd been so calm and cooperative in the past.

Dr. John's body was never found, but many presumed that he had perished in the fire. Government officials decided to scour the woods a second time, but never found him and figured he had died on the way out. They knew he was sick with nerve gas and that it would have taken a virtual miracle for him to survive such an onslaught of chemicals.

As for Clarence, he and his wife decided that it was time to move into a new home, given that their existing one was simply too small for their family of four. Now considerably richer, given their new partnership with the U.S. government, they chose to purchase a two-story home on Star Island and took great pleasure in standing outside their bedroom veranda, looking out on the water as the yachts and ships glided by on glittering waves of blue.

Clarence made it a habit to come home during the day around lunchtime, as his wife typically worked out at the gym in the morning and lunched with her friends at one of the trendy restaurants in town. With his children in school, these private lunches gave him time to unwind with a nice big salad in front of the television. Clarence didn't admit it to anyone, but he sometime watched porn during lunch, and masturbated with pleasure watching a little girl-on-girl action. It was another way to relax and be able to return to the office with a clear mind.

On one particular Wednesday, after a relatively tame morning in the office, Clarence pulled into the driveway in front of his home. He sighed happily and looked forward to the Cobb salad that the maid had prepared for him.

As he got out of the car, Clarence suddenly felt strange — almost as if someone was watching him. He quickly looked around the front of his house, but didn't see anything out of the ordinary, so decided it was just his imagination.

Stepping into the vast two-story home, he stopped to admire the landscape. The house was built like a glass fortress, with dark marble flooring, raised ceilings, and glass windows covering the exterior, giving way to a spectacular view of the water. When the sun was just right, it shot through the windows, casting a brilliant glow.

Yet despite the beautiful afternoon, Clarence didn't want to spend too much time admiring the view.

He was hungry.

And horny.

He decided to watch a bit of his favorite internet adult channel and then settle down for the salad once his sexual appetite was sated. Settling down in his office chair, he leaned back comfortably and turned on the laptop that was resting on the desk. Within seconds, he had lesbian scenes playing on the monitor.

Pulling down his pants and underwear, Clarence began to stroke himself as he watched the women moan and excite each other. He was getting close to orgasm, when a noise upstairs distracted him.

It sounded like someone had dropped something on the floor in his bedroom.

Turning off the computer, Clarence put his aching penis back in his underwear, wincing.

Damn, I hate blue balls, he thought. But his mind was already focused on what might be happening upstairs.

Concerned that someone might be trying to break into his house, Clarence walked over to the safe he had hidden near a bookshelf and opened it quickly. Inside he kept a loaded revolver, ready for any possible intruders. Unsure as to whether or not he was overreacting, he figured that carrying it upstairs was probably a wise move.

Walking over to the stairwell, Clarence decided to check to see if maybe the sounds were being made by the housekeeper or someone who had a key. He didn't want to wave a gun around unnecessarily.

"Hello?" he called out. "Is anyone up there?"

Nobody responded.

Clarence decided it was worth going upstairs to take a look around.

Ascending the staircase, he purposefully took harsh, loud steps to give a thief plenty of notice and the opportunity to escape.

No one jumped out at him. No one appeared.

Once he reached the second-floor landing, Clarence craned his neck to see if anything seemed strange. The house felt empty and yet, he couldn't shake the eerie feeling that remained.

He began to search the second floor by carefully peering around every corner and jumping into the center of each room, with his gun pointed straight ahead. By the time he'd done this same move several times, he felt a bit ridiculous.

Stepping back out into the hallway, he relaxed. No one was in the house.

And yet...

A sound caught his attention. He ran to his bedroom in time to see a person, dressed in a black wetsuit, open the large sliding glass doors that led out to the balcony and then slam them shut.

He watched in shock as the intruder appeared to lock the windows from the outside by sticking a large crowbar into the slider.

The intruder then did a swan dive off the balcony into the waters below and disappeared from view.

As Clarence stood in his bedroom, he remembered that he was holding a gun and ran toward the glass doors when suddenly, the bedroom door behind him slammed shut.

Whipping his head around, he raced for the door and turned the knob. The knob turned but when he tried to push the door open, it wouldn't budge. He pointed the gun at the knob, trying to shoot it off, but was unsuccessful and the bullet bounced off the metal, flying back at him.

Ducking, he managed to avoid the bullet and was about to shove himself against the door again, when something else caught his attention.

It was the TV inside of his bedroom. Somehow, the intruder had turned it on and the DVD player was gently humming. The screen was black but a few moments later, a smiling face emerged in front of him.

It was April, Dr. Johns' assistant.

How had she escaped? He wondered.

Her face smiled at him and when she began to speak, Clarence felt the panic build within…

"Hello there, Clarence. Remember me? You should. You gave specific instructions that I be strangled and left at the bottom of the fucking ocean. Too bad for you that you hired one of my distant cousins to do the job," she smiled and continued. "Yes. You heard me correctly. You hired one of my cousins to kill me. Luckily, I've got a close family."

April lifted a glass of wine to her lips and delicately sipped. When she spoke again, her eyes were sad. "After I escaped, the first place I needed to get to was the Illusions building. I needed to save as many people as possible. People we experimented on…people who never had a chance. Can't even remember how I got there…there are many different routes you can take…but just as I got close… you'll never believe who I saw…"

She paused…

"Yes, I found my mentor, Dr. Dan Johns lying on the side of the road. He was barely able to speak or move thanks to your master plan. And…he…died." She was crying now, tears falling down her cheeks.

"We had just pulled up to the hospital, when he had a seizure. He died in my arms. It was the worst experience of my life. We couldn't try to get help at the hospital because I knew it was too dangerous. So I brought him somewhere where I knew his body could be cremated and no one would know."

She glared at the camera and appeared to be shooting a piercing stare directly at Clarence.

"You killed him. You killed all of those innocent people just to create biological weapons. You did it without any remorse or pity. You're a monster."

April paused and then lifted up a canister. Clarence's blood chilled. He knew exactly what she was holding.

It was a gas canister.

"I've had to change my name, my identity…my life. It hasn't been easy. But while I've been transforming, some people have helped me. And they've helped me with all of this too. There's an old saying Clarence. What goes around, comes around. Right now, you're standing in a room that's been fitted with a tiny gas pipe. Look around, Clarence. Can you see it?"

Clarence looked around wildly.

Where the hell is it?

He was standing on the bed looking up at the ceiling when April continued.

"There's a reason you can't see it. We've hidden it far away where you can't reach it. In just a few moments, deadly nerve gas...the gas you had us test...will shoot out of that pipe and fill your room. Actually...it might already be starting to fill the air."

As Clarence began to pound on the door, April laughed as if she knew exactly what he'd be doing. "You can't get out. You can't escape. The maid has the day off. The phones have been disconnected. Your gun won't be able to shatter hurricane-proof windows and you only have one bullet so use it wisely. And, if we planned it correctly...let me guess... you didn't bring your cell phone upstairs did you? Nah, you left it on the table while you jerked off."

She stopped and sighed. "Oh, and one more thing. As you get really sick and start to die...just remember that you brought this on yourself. And you deserve to rot in the pits of hell. This one's for Dan."

She gave one last look at the camera and then shut off the recording. As the DVD came to an end, it began at the beginning again.

Clarence shut off the player and pointed his gun at the glass doors.

Click.

No bullets were left. He'd wasted his one chance at freedom by shooting at a doorknob.

Clarence sat down on the edge of his bed. He watched, almost with casual disinterest, as smoke filled the air and tickled his throat. The muscles in his legs began twitching and then with a stifled gasp, he dropped his head into his hands and began to cry.

———————

A half hour later, loud *booms* shook the elite neighborhood. Clarence Diamond's home exploded as a series of carefully placed bombs erupted one after the other. The job had been handled by professionals, and they left very few remains. Everything, including April's DVD, burned in a strategically set fire that ripped through the building and destroyed everything in its path.

Hundreds of miles away, April sat on a veranda as the cruise ship made its way across the Atlantic, headed for the Bahamas. She stared at the deep blue waves that seemed to go on for miles, creating hypnotic rhythms while the sun danced along the edges.

She was weeping softly, remembering the man who had taught her so much. She'd loved Dan from the start, but never told him. And now—it was too late.

Remembering that fateful night, she recalled how she had found her mentor...

He was lying on the side of the road, barely breathing. Gently picking him up, she managed to somehow drag him to the backseat of her car and laid him across the seat.

Dan woke for just a brief moment and stared at her, giving a small smile.

"Good...good to see you..." he had whispered. Then, his eyes had closed again.

She'd raced to the nearest hospital, which was still more than five miles away and tried to keep the conversation going. Even though he hadn't answered her, she knew that he could hear her in some distant recess of his mind.

When her car pulled up to the emergency room entrance, she'd gotten in the backseat and tried to lift him.

But Dan wouldn't move. Instead he opened his eyes again and whispered, "It's too late."

"No, no…"she'd cried, but stopped when he weakly put his hand on her arm.

"Don't cry. We did our best. Don't forget me…"

He closed his eyes as the shaking began…

Sighing, April looked at the canister in her hands. It was the same canister she'd been holding in the video. Only it hadn't been holding gas—it was holding Dan's cremated remains.

She said a quick and quiet prayer and then opened the lid, allowing the contents to escape. The dust flowed out quickly and seamlessly—floating into the air for a moment—and then landing gently amongst the waves.

A small smile on her lips, April tossed the empty canister overboard. She looked back one more time at the brilliant view and closed her eyes while the sun kissed her skin with the promise of a better future.

ABOUT THE AUTHOR

Sara Brooke is an Amazon bestselling author of horror, paranormal romance, and suspense fiction.

A lifelong avid reader of all things scary, Sara's childhood dream was to write books that make readers sleep with their lights on. She hopes that isn't too troubling for the thousands of readers worldwide who have purchased her books.

Sara has been published alongside horror legends Clive Barker and John Carpenter. She has written ten novels, and numerous novellas and short stories.

Sara resides in beautiful South Florida. She can be reached via her website at www.sarabrooke.com. Sara welcomes feedback and questions from readers.

Bibliography

Novels
Cursed Casino

Gardens of Babylon
Kransen House
Renovation
Still Lake
Sunken Park
The Bloodmane Chronicles
The Inn and Other Dark Tales
The Island
The Zyne Project

Novellas and Short Stories
Bathroom (Short Story in Madhouse Anthology)
Doug (Short Story)
Famine (Short Story in Anthology including stories from Clive
Barker & John Carpenter – currently in film development)
Ghost Swim (Short Story)
Mad Monkey King (Short Story)
Stairwell (Short Story)
The Bed (novella)
The Field (Short Story)
Vicious Circle (Short Story in Vicious Circle Anthology)

Curious about other Crossroad Press books? Stop by our website: http://crossroadpress.com
We offer quality writing
in digital, audio, and print formats.

Subscribe to our newsletter on the website homepage and receive a free eBook.